The Changing Man

**

KD BRADLEY

Best wishes

KD Bradley

First Edition

ISBN: 978-1-5272-5729-0

First published in Great Britain in 2020

Printed by Fine Print Services Ltd, Witney, Oxfordshire
fineprint.co.uk

All characters and other entities appearing in this work are **fictitious**. Any resemblance to real **persons**, dead or alive, or other real-life entities, past or present, is purely coincidental.

Part 1

Chapter 1

Daniel

Eight-year-old Daniel Edgar lay on his bed, sore from the welts left by his father's belt. He had overslept by five minutes, making him late for breakfast – the welts were a mark of his father's anger.

Daniel tried not to give his father the satisfaction of tears; had taken it like a man until he got to the sanctuary of his room, where he finally unleashed his emotions.

Half an hour later, his mother tiptoed into the room. She rushed to him, kissing his head and soothing him, softly crying.

"Why did you have to be late?" she whispered. "You know how mad that makes him."

She gave Daniel some paper and pencils, saying, "Maybe you can do some drawing?"

Not wanting to linger too long, Mary Edgar quickly soothed the angry welts on her son's back and buttocks with a cloth soaked in warm water and vinegar, then left him to continue soaking his pillow with hot, angry tears.

He wished he had never been born.

Daniel tried hard to keep to his father's ridiculously strict rules and regulations. Slipping up would always result in the same treatment and there was nothing he could do about it. He sought solace in art, his mind diverted by creating beauty on a page. A landscape. A bowl of fruit. A portrait. Anything. It was a welcome distraction and as time went by Daniel got better and better at his art.

∞

Never an academic, Daniel struggled through school and was glad to leave as soon as he was able. He joined the army to get away from his father's rigid routines – only to find he was now following those set down by the army.

At least there would be no more beatings with that damn belt. Daniel had taken it with him when he left and with great delight had thrown it out of the train window on his way to the training camp. As he watched the weapon that had scarred him as a child disappear from view, he felt a sense of calm release wash over him.

He enjoyed his military career to begin with. Having been brought up in such a regimented household, Daniel took to army life.

His kit was kept immaculate, boots shone to the highest of standards, uniform perfectly pressed, hair kept short and neat and he was clean shaven. He was a model recruit and the envy of other men who struggled to keep up with the army's high standards. Daniel enjoyed the training: rifle training, shooting, fitness, running with heavy kit bags, crossing rivers, setting up camps, deciphering codes.

He loved all of it and he was doing well, fitting in.

His first tour of duty was in Northern Ireland; the days of The Troubles were long gone but the presence of the British Army still ruffled feathers among the locals. Memories of some of the atrocities were still fresh in people's minds, in particular Bloody Sunday, when thirteen people were killed and fifteen wounded after members of the British Parachute Regiment opened fire on civil rights demonstrators in the Bogside.

The shootings led to widespread anger in Ireland and further afield; victims' families waited 47 years for prosecutions. There was enough evidence to prosecute only one paratrooper for only two of the murders so it was understandable that emotions still ran high in some quarters. The sight of the military was enough to cause anger and unease. Justice had not been served and the death of the innocent still weighed heavy in people's hearts.

Although the British Army did not have a heavy presence now, people still felt resentment they were there at all.

Soldiers were warned to be vigilant when out as civilians. All had fabricated stories of why they and their families were there and were forbidden to discuss anything military in public places for their own protection and the protection of other servicemen and women.

Most of the soldiers found it too hard to pretend to be someone they were not and kept their socialising among themselves.

Daniel kept his head down and got on with his duties, which mainly consisted of working alongside the local constabulary and engaging in personal development programmes.

During his frequent down time, he honed his skills as an artist, delighting the other soldiers with portraits of them and their girlfriends, the latter sketched from photographs and given as gifts.

Everyone was in awe of Daniel's artistic talent. He had vastly improved over the years and loved nothing more than sketching, losing himself in his artwork.

Now he had some money he treated himself to an easel and proper oil-based paints, which made his artwork come alive. He was grateful for this talent.

∞

Daniel's next and last tour was to Afghanistan; so different from peacetime Northern Ireland. It was so foreign to him, Daniel often wondered what the hell they were doing there, among people with such deep rooted radical ideas and such a different belief system.

Their methods of retribution were of biblical proportions, barbaric, outdated and ruthless. Punishments included stoning, flogging, caning, blinding, beheading, crucifixion and death by burning, all horrendous but still happening with alarming regularity. It was terrifying being there and knowing that, if captured, a fate such as those could befall you. Leniency and empathy were non-existent. More than ever, soldiers relied on one another for their safety, sanity and support. It didn't serve to be a loner; working as a team was a matter of survival.

No two days were ever the same in the Helmand province, which Daniel found disconcerting. Everything was unpredictable: events, people, landscapes and plans. Daniel found it hard to function without a strict routine and slowly, over time, his mental health deteriorated.

Feelings of chaos, disorder, not being in control, fear and anxiety all played a part. Daniel hid the conflicts in his mind and tried to continue being a productive serviceman. But inside he was falling apart.

During the evenings Daniel continued to find solace in his painting. It took his mind off the horror of Afghanistan during wartime. He cheered up his comrades with sketches of the Taliban in ridiculous situations, which delighted them.

He also produced many portraits of the local people, children, farmers, landscapes and animals; he built up quite a portfolio during the long evenings in Helmand.

The Taliban were a cowardly enemy, rarely seen. It was as

though the bushes themselves were firing at them. Six months' tour of duty sounds like a short time but thinking you could die at any moment made every day interminably long. One of the soldiers' duties was to train up the local police. Daniel heard just before he arrived that one of them had turned rogue and shot five men with one of their own weapons before being shot dead; the people the army were trying to help were murdering them.

IEDs (improvised explosive devices), usually planted at roadsides, were the biggest cause of fear. There had been many deaths and multiple amputees whose limbs were blown apart by these homemade, crude devices. Every journey made by the soldiers incorporated a fear of going over an IED. There were also ruthless snipers who attacked randomly when the soldiers were helping locals or when they were having some downtime playing football with local children. The Taliban did not care if they hit the local people or children.

One of the worst things about being in Afghanistan was the fact that everyone at home seemed oblivious to the horrors that were unfolding. People at home lived normally, going to the shops, going out for dinner and playing games consoles. It felt as though no one was supporting, encouraging or even grateful for the work the army was doing. Most people seemed to believe the army shouldn't be there at all and that made being there during such horrific times even harder.

Unlike previous wars, when everyone was involved with the war effort, this war felt like a private one between the soldiers and the Taliban. Coming back to Civvy Street was extremely difficult for a lot of men, who felt isolated and found it hard to integrate back into society.

Daniel's nerves were fraught after one young soldier was left an amputee after an IED exploded as he travelled through Helmand. The poor boy was in a terrible state and it was thought he might not pull through.

"Do you not think we are all terrified?" Private Smith asked one night when Daniel was visibly shaking. "Look mate, we just have to get on with the job and pray we come back alive. Hang in there, we'll get through this together."

One night, Daniel's insecurities and inner turmoil had a devastating effect on him and the men in his company. In a small village they searched houses for weapons, Taliban informants and members. The atmosphere became increasingly intense as everyone they encountered began to look suspiciously like a Taliban member – the Taliban had members as young as four years old.

Daniel's regiment were on full alert; just as they had been since they'd arrived. The nerves set off anxiety attacks and depression in some men, including Daniel. Droplets of sweat threatened to blind him as they searched house after house; he heaved audible sighs of relief when each house was cleared and the families were allowed to carry on their routines.

There were only two houses left to search. Daniel was sent upstairs in the first, where he gingerly looked through closets, drawers, under the beds and under the floorboards.

Suddenly, he heard a car approaching at speed; he froze as he heard the doors open.

There were running footsteps, gunshots – but he couldn't move. More vehicles pulled up, voices raised in fear, the sounds of... whoever it was leaving and a car speeding off. Carefully, Daniel made his way back downstairs.

Four of his comrades were dead. One had been hanged. There was blood everywhere. Daniel snatched up a wad of material and pushed it onto the gaping wound of a soldier who seemed to be still breathing, securing it with ripped sheets wrapped round the lad's body.

The injured soldier's eyes fluttered open. "Where the hell were you?" he whispered, then fell deeper into unconsciousness. Help arrived quickly and the wounded soldier was taken to the field hospital.

Back at base, Daniel was interviewed extensively, the only witness able to reveal what had happened. In his report, Daniel outlined the speed of events, that he had been unable to do anything to help his comrades, that approaching vehicles must have scared off the enemy before they could come upstairs and find him.

There was speculation that Daniel could have done something to save at least some of the men but with no other witnesses there was no evidence to keep the inquiry going. The case was closed, with the recommendation that Daniel be released from his duties in Helmand. The wounded soldier remained in a coma and was not expected to make it.

Daniel readily accepted his voluntary discharge from the army. He was deemed a liability, failing to come to the aid of his team on that fateful night. In the circumstances, it was agreed discharge was the best course of action for all involved. Daniel could not have been more relieved. He never wanted to see Afghanistan again in his life; but what would he do without the army?

Chapter 2

Reggie

The youngest of a family of seven, Reggie was the proverbial bad apple. From a young age he was a boisterous troublemaker and very sneaky. He would often get his siblings into trouble for something that he had done. At first his parents were oblivious, not for one minute thinking their precious Reggie would be so devious. But when eventually he was caught out, from then on he fooled no one.

He was a charming wee boy, with thick dark hair, brown eyes and round, rosy cheeks. People often commented on his good looks and he often got away with murder because of them.

To begin with, his troublemaking ways were fairly harmless. He'd steal a cigarette from his dad's packet and the blame would lay with Tommy, his older brother, who openly smoked in the house. When money started to go missing from his mother's purse – a fiver here, a fiver there – the finger of blame was pointed at his sister Denise. She was always wanting new clothes for the disco on a Saturday night. Denise protested her innocence but it fell on deaf ears. Everyone suspected it was her who stole the money.

Fed up, Denise set a trap and caught Reggie red handed one morning as he dipped into his mother's purse. Caught off guard, he made up a story about needing the money to help out a desperate friend, whose mother had just died of cancer. The sympathy card worked and he was off the hook for a bit.

But now his family were wary of him and he had to lie low with his antics until the heat wore off.

Reggie kept his head down and was good as gold for the next few months. Soon after, his mother's sister died suddenly of a heart attack. His parents were devastated. The funeral was arranged and after the church service there was tea and sandwiches at the local bowling club.

Mourners gathered in groups chatting, some drinking tea, some preferring to hit the bar for a stiff drink. Reggie surveyed the room. On almost every chair, bags lay open and abandoned, men's coats hung unattended on the backs of chairs… easy targets. Reggie went around the room pinching from every available pocket or purse until his pockets were bulging. He was becoming quite the thief.

Reggie was pleased with himself as the family arrived home. He hid the stash under a loose floorboard in the bedroom he shared with his brothers. That night, the doorbell rang – it was Bob from the bowling club. Reggie listened hard from his bedroom.

"Hi, sorry to bother you, Mr Brown. We've had a number of people complaining they've had money stolen at the funeral this afternoon. Did you or Mrs Brown have anything taken? I'm trying to get an idea of the extent of the robberies before going to the police to report it." Bob sounded exhausted, as he shared the news standing on the doorstep.

"Come in," Reggie heard his father say, while he sat panicking in his room. "Maggie, come here," called out Mr Brown. "Bob's saying that folks had money nicked at the funeral today. Can you check your purse to see if anything's missing? I'll check my jacket."

Reggie heard the high-pitched voice of his mother. "No, no I've not got anything missing, Bob. This is terrible. Have you any idea who would do such a thing?"

"Perhaps we should go into the kitchen where we can talk in private," said Bob.

Once the door was shut Reggie could hear no more but he had a sinking feeling he'd once again been caught in the act. Two minutes later he heard his father jump out of his seat and swing open the kitchen door violently.

"Reggie Raymond Brown, get your backside down here now!" his father's voice boomed.

Anticipating what was about to happen, Reggie grabbed the money and chucked some clothes in an old holdall before escaping out of the bedroom window. Reggie ran and ran, never looking back. He knew his father would have his guts for garters and that it would be unforgiveable to have been caught stealing at his beloved aunt's funeral. Reggie knew he could never go home.

He caught a train to London and lived on the streets for a while, begging and dossing down wherever he could. It was a frightening time but he grew up fast and learned to take care of himself. His good looks went a long way during these tough days; he would help old ladies carry their bags home and they would give him some money for doing so. He would help them into their homes and pinch whatever he could find of value.

At 17 he looked older than his years and was able to get into pubs and clubs. He was popular with the ladies, who were unaware of his vagabond lifestyle. Having spruced himself up by pinching clothes in the shopping centre, Reggie scrubbed up well and no one would have guessed his status in life. He never had any bother getting a girl. He just didn't want to keep them and only ever had one night stands, involving heavy petting and sometimes more. He always stole the contents of the girl's purse, putting the money in his pocket the next morning.

When he turned 18, he joined the army – a home at last and comrades he considered his new family. Reggie adapted well to army life. No one knew his shady background and he came across as an honest, hardworking individual. There would be no thieving here – Reggie could not afford to get kicked out and lose the only family he now had.

On his third tour of Afghanistan, Reggie was involved in the search for weapons in a small village in Helmand, along with five other servicemen. With only two homes left to search, the group were attacked when the enemy burst in through the door, firing weapons. One man was upstairs and, to Reggie's dismay, did not come down and attack from above. Reggie lay bleeding heavily, faking at being dead until the gang were scared off by approaching vehicles. When the soldier upstairs finally came down and attended to his wounds, Reggie stared into his face and took a mental picture. "Where the hell were you?" he whispered, before falling into a coma.

When Reggie woke from his coma six months later, he found out that Daniel Edgar was the only other surviving soldier from that fateful night; all the others had died from their wounds. Reggie was devastated. Two of these men had been like brothers to him. He heard that Daniel had been voluntarily discharged on the basis that there were no other witnesses and his story of everything happening so fast had been accepted.

Reggie knew that there had been time and that Daniel could have saved the day if he hadn't been such a coward. He was furious at the injustice of it. He recovered from the coma, his wounds healed but the mental scars of that night haunted him. Reggie had witnessed a lot during his tours of Helmand: the devastation IEDs caused, young servicemen, with their lives in front of them, lying screaming in agony, with devastating wounds, in the pit of despair. Snipers attacked them while they were helping locals build hospitals and schools; even rogue policemen turned on them when they were trying to train them. The injustice played over and over in Reggie's mind.

∞

Reggie's anxiety and depression had a detrimental effect on his ability to concentrate. He was unpredictable and the men didn't want him on any missions where he could cause a problem. His condition was impossible to hide from the hierarchy and it was soon common knowledge that Reggie was suffering from PTSD. After a complete psychological assessment, he was deemed unfit for duty. Reggie's Commanding Officer broke the news but Reggie pleaded with him, saying that he would get help and be back to normal; but the Commanding Officer was unbreakable in his decision. Reggie memorised his face, his eyes full of hate for the man who seemed to have no qualms in getting him medically discharged.

As Reggie packed his gear, he felt a blackness rising in his soul.

Away from the army, Reggie soon went back to his vagabond ways, unable to hold down a job or a girlfriend. He preferred to live on the streets, unattached and unburdened by anyone. He was fuelled by thoughts of rage and revenge – but he was going to take his own sweet time about it.

Chapter 3

Daniel & Anna

Daniel found it difficult returning to normality. He decided to retrain as an accountant and thought he would like to work for a non-profit organisation. He undertook an undergraduate degree, with coursework in finance and accounting on a two-year accounting associate degree. He made some new friends on the course and enjoyed socialising with them at the weekends. They usually hung out at a bar called Finnegan's, a rough and tumble type place where you could play pool and darts and which had the occasional live band in the evenings. It was low key and understated and suited Daniel perfectly. He didn't expect or aim to meet any girls there; and then he met the love of his life.

A local band happened to be playing on the Friday night. They were doing covers of The Jam and The Who, going down well with everyone, and people were up dancing. Daniel was there with a few of his mates from the course, when he spotted a gorgeous, petite brunette dancing with her friends. She had small features, and big brown eyes with cleverly done, sultry make-up and a hint of cat's eye.

Daniel couldn't take his eyes off her and when his friends noticed how distracted he was, they insisted he buy her a drink. Normally quite reserved, Daniel knew he might never see her again if he didn't make a move so, with some Dutch courage, on he went. She was even more beautiful close up. Her name was Anna Jones. She was originally from Wales but was in Yorkshire training to be a hairdresser. They hit it off and soon became inseparable.

Daniel told her briefly about his time in the army but never went into too much detail. Anna sensed it was difficult for him to open up and never pushed the subject. She was totally in love with Daniel. Having had boyfriends in the past, Anna was ready to settle down. She longed for a family and a happy home life and this was partly why she had chosen to be a hairdresser. She figured that, when she had children, she could still fit her job in with childcare and would not have to rely on anyone to look after her kids. She had seen how difficult it was for her older sister Carys, when she had her children and wanted to go back to work. More often than not, their parents would look after the children. Anna did not want to burden them with even more grandparenting. She saw it all the time – grandparents being relied on too heavily to help with their offsprings' children. She felt it was unfair and too much for some of them; though she understood some people had no choice.

She had always wanted to be a stay-at-home mum and bring up her children, her way, without relying on anyone. Anna had always hated asking for help. She had been quite independent from a young age, which was why she had chosen to study in Yorkshire instead of Wales. She wanted to live alone for a bit, away from her mother's apron strings, though she was close to her parents and loved them dearly.

After only a few months of dating, Anna found she was staying at Daniel's flat more than her own.

"Why don't you move in?" Daniel asked her sleepily one morning. Anna was getting ready to go to college.

"Don't you think it's a bit soon?" she asked but her eyes were shining at the prospect.

"I miss you when you're not here, can't bear to be without you for longer than five minutes, so it makes sense, right?" said Daniel. He opened his arms and Anna ran into them for a hug.

"I'd love it," she gleamed happily. "As long as you're sure, I'm all for it."

That day, Daniel helped Anna cart all of her belongings – mostly clothes, a lamp and a few cuddly toys – from her home to his flat. They celebrated with a Chinese takeaway and a bottle of wine. They were both beyond happy.

Daniel found himself enjoying his course and managing the work better than he had expected. Anna was showing a natural talent for hairdressing and enjoying it thoroughly. Over time, Daniel had gone with Anna home to her parents and he had immediately got along well with them and her sister Carys,

Carys's husband Ben and the kids, Sophia and Sam. He felt at ease there. They were all very warm, welcoming people. The kids were bundles of fun and Daniel loved play fighting with them, taking them to the swing park with Anna and treating them to ice cream. They doted on him. It made Daniel realise he would love to have children of his own. He was so in love with Anna he decided she was definitely the one and why waste time? He knew he wanted to marry her and begin their lives together.

Before they left to go back to Yorkshire, Daniel went for a walk with Bill, Anna's father.

"Bill, I know you've only known me a relatively short space of time, but why am I so nervous?" Daniel laughed, moving about from one foot to another. "Anyway I'm just going to come out with it. Would you allow me to propose to Anna?" He closed his eyes, waiting on Bill's response.

"Well, I can't say I'm surprised," said Bill in his thick Welsh accent. "It is quite soon. I can see how happy you both are. You have my blessing. Just you make sure you look after my girl with your life. I never want to see her unhappy on account of anything you have done. Can you promise me that you will always put her happiness first?" Bill was looking questioningly at Daniel, his face stone set.

"Absolutely," Daniel concurred, "I give you my solid word that I will always put her happiness before my own. I'm so pleased you agreed. I'm planning a romantic meal next weekend, when I'll propose. I've still got to buy the ring. I've seen one she loves, she pointed it out one day on a walk, in an antique dealer's window." Daniel was getting more and more animated as they walked and Bill had a chuckle to himself. He was delighted his daughter had found someone she really loved. They agreed to keep quiet about the whole thing when they got back to the house but gave each other conspiratorial winks throughout the rest of the evening.

∞

Daniel and Anna's wedding was beautiful, held in the church that Anna and her family had attended all their lives. The church was a quaint little place with beautiful gardens for the photographs. Daniel's parents attended, his father an old man now. He had softened with age but Daniel still remembered the beatings and had never grown close to him. For his mother's sake he tolerated him. As Daniel waited for his bride at the altar, he could not have been happier. The Wedding March played and he could not resist looking behind him as Anna and her father walked down the aisle. She was breathtakingly beautiful, in a full-length, white dress made of delicate lace, complete with a tiara and veil.

"You look beautiful," Daniel whispered as she joined him at the altar. Anna's eyes were aglow with happiness. Her dark hair was swept high in a flattering bun, with wisps flowing down in a romantic fashion. The service was short and heartfelt. Afterwards there was a reception in a local hotel, where they all enjoyed a scrumptious meal. Daniel could not have been prouder as he led Anna on to the dance floor for their first dance, 'You are the sunshine of my life' by Stevie Wonder.

"I hope we'll always be this happy," said Anna as they swayed around the dance floor.

"Of course we will," Daniel assured her. "Thank you for making me the happiest man alive."

Chapter 4

Anna

At first Daniel and Anna were blissfully happy. They quickly fell into a routine and were over the moon when, six months later, Anna fell pregnant with their first child. Daniel could not have been more attentive, treating her like a china doll; he was almost too much. Anna found it endearing.

Happily, she gave birth to Leah successfully and without any complications, early one autumn morning. Parenthood was exhausting, as the young couple soon found. Their previous easy routine soon went out of the window as they sleepwalked through their days, having been up all night with Leah. She was a normal baby, waking every three to four hours for a feed. Daniel would take his turn getting up to feed her, letting Anna sleep on. They worked well together, bringing up their baby. His family meant the world to him.

When Leah turned two, Anna found out she was expecting again. This time round, the couple were more laid back about the pregnancy and looked forward to the birth.

In the summer, Anna went into labour and six hours later gave birth to another little girl, whom they called Eloise. Anna felt fulfilled; she loved being a mother and doted on her girls. She was still able to keep up her hairdressing. Either clients came to her home or she would take the girls and go to theirs. Not once did Anna rely on babysitters. The girls were always by her side, just as she had planned from early on.

As time went by and the girls grew up, Anna noticed that their lives had somehow fallen into a very rigid routine. Daniel had become very regimented in his day-to-day activities. He laid down the law about what time meals were, chores, homework and bedtime. Anna was beginning to feel the whole thing rather stifling. She felt stuck, frustrated and had no idea how to go about creating a more carefree lifestyle for them. She had a couple of good girlfriends, Rachel and Susan, whom she met once a week. She loved the easy flow of their friendship; they usually drank too much, said too much, danced too much but they always had a good time.

"I don't want to sound ungrateful," Anna confided to them during a girls' night out. "I'm really bored with the routine Daniel's got us all sticking rigidly to. How do I get us out this rut?" Her pretty face fell in despair and after one too many wines her eyes filled with tears. The girls were used to hearing this. They'd been hearing it for a while now and they could see how unhappy Anna was becoming.

"Why don't you arrange a weekend away? Just you and Daniel?" Rachel suggested.

"Yes," enthused Susan. "That would be perfect, then you

could explain how you've been feeling. Give him a bit of love, sexy underwear, Kama Sutra and I'm sure he'll make some changes," she winked knowingly.

"Do you really think that would work?" Anna said, feeling suddenly optimistic. "You know, I would really love that. A break from the old routine might be just what we need." Happily, and a bit drunk, Anna went home. She'd have to wait until morning to suggest a weekend away; Daniel was already fast asleep.

Next morning, Anna didn't feel so brave about mentioning the weekend away. She knew Daniel hated disruption to his routine; she also felt that she could not go on like this. She bit the bullet.

"Daniel, how would you feel about the two of us getting away for a few days?" she piped up quickly before she talked herself out of it.

"What?" replied Daniel, taken aback but his mind immediately going through excuses. He hated going away, it meant their routine went out the window and the kids would be unsettled for weeks afterwards. "It's not a good time, work's really busy at the moment. Maybe some other time, when the girls are a bit older." He kissed her on the head, grabbing his coat as he made a quick exit. Anna felt deflated, all the hopes and plans made last night gone. She felt more trapped than ever.

Chapter 5

Daniel

Relief flooded through Daniel as he left the house. There was no way he wanted to go away for a weekend, leaving behind his girls and his routine. He led a regimented life, much like his father before him: leaving his house each morning at 7.35am to catch the 7.45am train into town; stopping at Sarah's Bakery to buy two bacon rolls, one for him and one for the homeless man on the corner, tucking the roll behind the homeless man's head before continuing to work; arriving home at 6pm every evening; eating with his family at 6.30pm; gardening after dinner to unwind; watching an hour or two of TV before bed.

The weekend schedule was different but still a routine. On Saturday mornings he took Anna to the supermarket and put a bet on at the local bookies. In the afternoon he watched sport on TV, ate dinner, watched a movie, perhaps had a few drinks.

Sunday was a family day; they'd all go out for a run and Sunday lunch. In the evening, Daniel would meet his mate Pete for a few drinks in the local pub. The routine rarely changed.

On Monday morning, his weekday routine started again, just the way he liked it.

But this morning... he left the house disconcerted by Anna's suggestion of a weekend away. He slotted into his routine again, visiting Sarah's Bakery and ordering two bacon rolls – but when he headed round the corner, the homeless man was not there. Daniel scanned the streets.

A commotion around the corner moved Daniel to investigate. A thug was viciously beating up the homeless man. Daniel stood staring, unable to take his eyes away from the scene. The homeless man caught his eye and the expression on his face was a plea for help.

But Daniel was going to be late for work. He didn't want to get involved. He turned away and strode to his office.

Next morning, Daniel bought a local newspaper for his commute. He scanned the pages for a report on the attack but there was nothing. He avoided the bakery and the homeless man. He took a different route to the office.

But the change to his routine unsettled him. He couldn't shake the feeling that something bad was about to happen to him. After avoiding the bakery, the corner and the homeless man for the rest of the week, Daniel decided it was time to go back to his usual routine.

∞

Monday morning. Daniel left home at 7.35am, caught the train at 7.45am. He visited Sarah's Bakery, ordered two bacon rolls. Hardly breathing, he made his way to the corner... and there was the homeless man, asleep in his usual spot. Daniel sighed with relief and leant forward to tuck the bacon roll behind the man's head.

As he withdrew his arm again, a strong hand gripped his wrist. Daniel jumped back but was held from moving further away. The homeless man's face emerged from under the grubby blanket. Daniel grimaced at the bruised, ugly markings, swollen eyes and fat lip.

"Why did you do nothing?" rasped the dishevelled man.

Daniel, suddenly sweating, tugged back his arm and turned to leave without replying. Without looking back, he headed straight to his office.

Shaking and nauseated, he asked himself, *why did I do nothing?* He knew the answer.

It would have upset his routine. He would have been late for work. He would have had to speak to the police and maybe end up involved in a court case, which could last months. That's why he did nothing.

Daniel couldn't face the homeless man again, not ever! His new routine left out Sarah's Bakery and the bacon rolls, for him as well as the homeless man. The different route unsettled Daniel but he figured he'd get used to it. It was worth it not to see the homeless man again. He settled into the new routine and tried to put the whole episode behind him.

Three weeks later, on a Monday morning, he stepped off

the train and walked to the exit. The homeless man appeared from nowhere and pushed an envelope into his hands, before disappearing into the crowds.

Startled, Daniel stuffed it into his pocket and made his way to the office. Once there, he trembled as he took out the envelope and ripped it open. The note inside read, "You stood by and watched me nearly die. Now I will stand by and watch you." Frantically, Daniel turned the note over but that was all it said. He read it again and again. What could it mean? He stared at his computer screen but could focus on nothing.

∞

Daniel's routine began to change. Every night, on the way home from work, he stopped at the local store and bought a bottle of vodka. He couldn't walk further than a few steps without looking over his shoulder. And after a while, his family begin to notice the change in him. He tried to hide his drinking but Anna was very aware of it and soon arguments became a regular occurrence in the Edgar household. The girls stayed in their rooms rather than spend time with him. No one wanted to go out for Sunday lunch any more.

Chapter 6

Anna & Reggie

Still reeling from Daniel's refusal to go away for a weekend, Anna noticed that Daniel had begun hitting the bottle and she was hurt by his secrecy.

She was relieved to meet Rachel and Susan for a night out. Rachel, being single, loved to drag the girls out to the local bar, where she sometimes hooked up with a lad at the end of the night. For the first time in her married life, Anna was envious of her friend's relationship status. She dressed in a pair of black jeans, heels, and a strappy top with blazer, smoky eyes make-up and a slash of red lipstick. Anna was unaware of how hot she looked, as she rang the doorbell to Rachel's flat.

Rachel answered the door and gave a low whistle. "Look at you!" she exclaimed. "You're going to pull all the men tonight looking like that, girlfriend," and she almost looked dismayed.

"As if," retorted Anna. "Anyway, one man is more than enough, thank you very much, even if he is a pain in the neck most of the time."

"Are you guys still having problems?" Rachel asked as she poured them both a drink.

"Well, he flat out refused the weekend away. It's impossible to hold him down for a conversation. His routine is so rigid he doesn't even have time to talk. He's also been drinking heavily, which is not like him. Anyway, let's forget my problems for one night. I want to get him out of my head and enjoy myself for once."

"Here's to that," said Susan, who had arrived in time to hear the end of the conversation, and grabbed the drink offered by Rachel's outstretched hand. "I'm in the mood for a good night, too," she added. "Tom's being a pain as well. Do men get periods? 'Cos he's been acting like he's got premenstrual cramps for the last fortnight," she laughed. The girls discussed Tom for a bit, while Rachel finished getting ready and they had several more drinks before hitting the local bar.

On entering the bar, the music was pumping, a local band playing covers. Straight away, already slightly drunk, the girls ditched their bags and coats and hit the dance floor. The attractive threesome turned heads, and men and women alike watched them cavort on the dance floor with looks of admiration, jealousy and pure fascination. This was just what Anna needed; a night out with her best friends, letting her hair down and not caring about Daniel, just for one night. As they continued to down drinks, dance and flirt, the evening passed quickly. Pretty soon, Rachel had her eyes on a man by the bar, and flirted outrageously with him. Before anyone knew what was happening, she was snogging his face off. Susan and Anna looked on in mock horror, though they had seen Rachel do this on many occasions. Anna was surprised by a feeling of envy at her friend's freedom; she shook her head to rid herself of the sensation.

As Susan and Anna hit the dance floor once more, Anna felt the burn of a man's gaze on her. Her eyes were drawn to his, as he stood admiring her, propped up by the bar. He had a rugged handsomeness and she was attracted to him from the word go. Susan saw the connection and encouraged her to go and ask him for a dance.

"Go on, Anna, go have some fun, what happens in the bar stays in the bar, right?" she laughed before heading off to the ladies. Anna carried on dancing by herself but held the stranger's gaze. He eventually approached her, just as the song changed to a slow one. He grabbed Anna by the waist and held her in a tight embrace as they swayed to the music. He smelled her hair and closed his eyes.

"Oh my God, you smell as good as you look," he whispered into her ear. He sucked her earlobe, and Anna felt her knees weaken with desire. As they gazed at each other she was lost in the beauty of his dark brown eyes. Before she knew it, he was kissing her and she was kissing him back, hungrily, passionately.

"Let's get out of here," he said, grabbing her hand tightly. As if in a trance, Anna grabbed her coat and bag and managed to tell Rachel she was going. Rachel, too involved in snogging her latest squeeze, acknowledged Anna was leaving and promised to let Susan know.

Once outside, the fresh air hit Anna and she felt even drunker than before but somehow exhilarated. The stranger pulled her down a dimly lit alleyway and they snogged for what seemed like an eternity. His hands expertly explored her body and it felt good. Anna let him do what he was doing and totally got caught up in the heat of the moment. Before she knew what was happening, she realised things were going too far. She did not want this.

"Stop," she said, at last coming to her senses. "I can't, I'm married. I'm sorry, I should never have let things go this far."

"Oh, I know you are," said the stranger. "That's why this is going to happen, whether you like it or not."

Anna immediately sobered up. "What do you mean?" she asked, trying to sit up – but he was too strong for her. Pushing her back and holding her down with a strength she could not match, the stranger continued. When he was done, Anna lay shivering, with tears and snot running down her face.

"Why?" she asked weakly. "I said no."

"You can ask your coward of a husband," the man spat back. He looked at her like she was a piece of dirt on the floor, his handsome features changed now to an expression of menace. Anna threw up where she lay. The man laughed nastily and left her.

Anna somehow made it home and sat in the shower for hours, before crawling into bed. Sleep did not come, and fear gripped her. This was not just a stranger. This was someone who knew Daniel and had used her as revenge. And, shamefully, she had let him.

∞

Although Anna had felt things could not get any worse for them, they managed to. Daniel had already been drinking heavily. They had been almost like strangers in their own home – and now this. He would never forgive her if he found out; and she could hardly forgive herself.

"Hey Susan, its Anna," she called her friend. "Can the kids and I come and stay with you for a while? Things have gotten pretty bad."

Chapter 7

Daniel

Anna had arrived home in a state on Saturday evening, after her night out with the girls. On Sunday she hardly spoke. Daniel had other things on his mind and barely noticed.

On Monday morning, Daniel left the house at 7.35am and caught his 7.45am train. His eyes bloodshot and his suit creased, an unshaven Daniel arrived at the office. His work had gone downhill since he received the ominous note and it had not gone unnoticed. His boss was waiting in his office for him.

"What's going on Daniel?" he asked, looking concerned. "Are you having problems at home; are Anna and the girls okay?"

"Yes, they are absolutely fine," Daniel confirmed. "We are all fine Tom, there's no problem."

"Then why has your work slipped so badly? You know we lost the Davidson contract last week because your figures were, well, quite frankly ridiculous?"

Tom went to the window and looked at the street below. "We can't afford to lose any clients, Daniel. We are a small company and if our competitors hear of any flaws they'll swoop in and eat us alive. I hate to do this, Daniel, but you've left me with no choice but to let you go. I'm sincerely sorry."

On the way home, Daniel stopped at the store for a bottle of vodka. It was 11.15am. He sat on a bench in the park with his head in his hands. He couldn't believe his life had spiralled so quickly out of control.

By the time he arrived home, Daniel was in a terrible state. "Anna," he slurred, "I'm home." His call echoed down the hallway, and he stood listening to the eerie silence that followed. The house seemed empty. Daniel stumbled upstairs and into his bedroom. He flung open the wardrobe doors and was horrified to see Anna's side nearly empty. He went to the girls' rooms and checked their wardrobes – they too were nearly empty. He fell to the floor and cried, deep, gut-wrenching sobs. In one day he had lost everything.

In a heap on the floor, he pulled out the note from his pocket and read it again. "You stood by and watched me nearly die. Now I will stand by and watch you." Furious, he crumpled the note and threw it towards the window – through which the face of the homeless man was staring at him. Daniel shut his eyes tight and when he opened them again the face was gone.

Daniel stumbled to his feet and made his way to the kitchen, pouring himself a large vodka and gulping it down in one go. He pulled open a drawer and took out a packet of painkillers, chucking them on the table. He began popping the pills and washing them down with the vodka. As his head became heavier, he slid from the chair to the floor.

Night fell, and Daniel remained in darkness on the kitchen

floor.

∞

A strong hand shook Daniel awake. His eyes fluttered open just as the homeless man thrust his fingers into Daniel's throat. Daniel gagged – then threw up.

When he had finished, he stared at the homeless man's face. "Why did you save me? You should have let me die," Daniel grunted.

"You really don't recognise me, do you?" The homeless man asked – but Daniel fell back into unconsciousness.

In the morning, they faced each other across the dining table.

"I'll ask you again," said Reggie. "You really don't recognise me, do you?" He stared pointedly into Daniel's face. Daniel stared back, taking in the man's features; he'd have been quite attractive if he were not so poorly groomed.

"No, I don't think so," replied Daniel, his brow creased in concentration.

Reggie continued, "I'll give you a clue: Afghanistan, village raid – ring any bells?"

Daniel lost what little colour he had left on his face as it dawned on him who the man was.

"You're the wounded man, left in a coma," he croaked.

"Well done," Reggie gave a mocking round of applause.

"Took you long enough to work that out. I was in a coma for six months. When I came round I had flashbacks of that night, anxiety attacks that spilled over into my working life. I tried to hide it but incident after incident didn't go unnoticed. Eventually I was forced to take medical discharge from the army. Ruined my life. I mean, how am I meant to fit back into society? That's why I've spent every day since then thinking about you – you are the reason this happened to me. If you hadn't been such a coward you could have saved some, if not all of our men. And me from being wounded," he added. "But you chose to cower upstairs."

Daniel began to protest.

"Now, we both know the truth," Reggie raised his voice. "If I hadn't been in a coma at your inquiry everyone would know and you'd probably be serving time for being a coward. And you know it."

Daniel was silent, thinking Reggie was probably correct. If the truth had been told he wouldn't have walked away with a voluntary discharge.

Reggie was angry now. "To add insult to injury you chose to watch me being beaten half to death on the street. Once a coward always a coward, eh? Is that it?"

"I couldn't get involved," Daniel replied, weakly. "My job… I'd have been late for work." Even as he said it, Daniel realised how lame it sounded. "I'm truly sorry, if it means anything to you." He felt the shame on his face.

"No. Sorry doesn't really cut it, Daniel. And no, it means nothing to me. Don't fret, though. I have something in mind that could make up for your cowardly past. Something you will do. And if you don't, I might have to drop by the Military Police to make a report about that night in Helmand, and it might mean they have to reopen the case, and that might mean you have to face trial. Even do some time."

Reggie was scaring him now; it was possible he would have to face a trial if the case was reopened.

"What is it you want me to do?" Daniel asked, resigned to the fact that he was being held over a barrel.

"You lost your job, right? I'm homeless, right? We're both financially screwed, would you agree?" Not waiting on a reply, Reggie continued, "I want you to commit a robbery."

Daniel opened his mouth to protest but Reggie continued. "There's an isolated place in the countryside, an old farmhouse. The person who lives there happens to own two paintings worth over a million pounds each. All you have to do is break in and steal them. Once you've got them, I'll take over selling them and we'll split the proceeds. Only then will I get out your life. Sound good?"

"No, it doesn't sound good," Daniel found his voice. "It sounds like a bloody nightmare."

"Nonetheless, you are doing this, Daniel. You owe me." Reggie rubbed his hands together. "Now, let me tell you what's going to happen."

Chapter 8

Reggie & Daniel

Reggie explained to Daniel that he'd been casing the farmhouse for several weeks and knew the old man's routine well. They decided the best night for the robbery would be a Saturday. Reggie told him the kitchen window was well worn and would be the easiest entrance point. The old man went to bed around 10pm, so Daniel would wait until after 11pm to make sure the man was asleep.

Reggie repeated that this was an opportunity for Daniel to prove he was not a coward; that they would both be very well off once the paintings were sold. Daniel felt sick to his stomach at the prospect of what he was about to do but felt he had no option; he was terrified of Reggie and believed he would actually kill him if he refused to take part.

Saturday night came round all too quickly. Daniel dressed head to foot in black, as Reggie insisted, and drove towards the secluded farmhouse. He parked about a mile from the house and walked the rest of the way. His breathing was fast and he was sweating profusely. He considered backing out but knew he couldn't and resigned himself to the fact that he had to do this if he wanted Reggie out of his life for good.

Arriving at the farmhouse, Daniel was relieved to see Reggie was correct about the kitchen window. He easily broke it open, climbed quietly through and stood in the middle of the kitchen. His breathing was laboured and he leaned against the sink for a few moments to steady himself.

Reggie said the paintings were hidden in a cupboard under the stairs, so Daniel, using the torch on his phone, made his way through to the hallway. He stopped to listen – no sound of the old man, so he continued to the cupboard under the stairs. He turned the handle to find the door locked.

"Damn," Daniel muttered under his breath. He returned to the kitchen to search the drawers for a key, when a light suddenly snapped on, blinding him for a second.

"Who are you?" The old man was standing in the doorway aiming a rifle at him. "And what are you doing on my property?"

Daniel slowly raised his hands, feeling almost relieved at being caught and not having to continue this hideous mission.

"Easy now," he whispered. "Please don't shoot. Let me explain. I have a bit of a story for you."

The old man motioned towards a chair, and Daniel moved slowly to sit down. The man managed to keep a firm grip on the rifle while tying Daniel's ankles and wrists to the chair.

"I'm all ears," he finally said, as he sat down on a chair close by.

Daniel poured out the whole story to the old man, being honest about his part in Afghanistan and describing how he had frozen in fear instead of heroically saving the day. He told him of Reggie's part in his downward spiral and how he had been blackmailed into this robbery.

The old man listened quietly to the story and seemed to think for a bit.

"This man, Reggie – what's his full name?" he asked.

"Reggie Raymond Brown," Daniel said, wearily.

"Ah, makes sense now," the old man told him. "I was his Commanding Officer in Helmand. He came to my attention a number of times after coming out of the coma; he showed signs of PTSD and was becoming a danger to himself and his unit. In fact, I was the one who insisted he be medically discharged. The day of his discharge he sought me out and told me that one day he would get his revenge. I just dismissed it as the ramblings of a mad man, because he was at that time quite mad."

Tears sprung to Daniel's eyes and he realised they were tears of relief.

"So. I'm Jack Blair," continued the old man, "and here is what we are going to do."

∞

At the end of his short speech, Jack handed Daniel a phone and untied his hands. Daniel called Reggie.

"There's a problem," Daniel said as soon as Reggie answered the phone. "I've killed the old man. It was an accident. I had to."

When he ended the call, he and Jack stared at each other and waited.

Before long, Reggie arrived at the farmhouse. Jack confronted him, pointing the gun at his head, and tied him up in the seat next to Daniel.

"I knew you were mad but not mad enough to dare steal from me," Jack told a stunned Reggie.

"You ruined my life," replied Reggie. "You and him, that bloody coward sitting there. You couldn't even get this right," he aimed at Daniel.

"I never wanted to get this right," replied Daniel. "I never wanted any part of this but you blackmailed me and I want you out my life."

"Shut it, both of you," Jack ordered. "Here's what's going to happen. Reggie, you think I've ruined your life but you were out of control in Helmand and you know it. If it hadn't been me signing your medical discharge papers it would've been some other officer, that's just fact. However, I am willing to compensate you somewhat generously if you agree to leave the country and set up home elsewhere and start a new life. You must never contact Daniel or me again. Do you accept?"

Reggie seemed shocked into silence. Perhaps he thought Jack would at least call the police, if he wasn't going to shoot him. After a moment he replied, "I think that's only fair. I've had no life since my discharge, so yes, I agree – if the compensation is adequate, I will leave and never return."

Daniel was looking with bafflement at both the men.

Jack untied Reggie and handed him a cheque. The younger man smirked as he pocketed it. "Oh, by the way, Daniel," he said. "Your wife's a hot piece of skirt."

"What the hell?" Daniel struggled to get loose from his binds.

"Yeah," continued Reggie, "send her my love will ya? Tell her I loved our night together but she should really get that tattoo on her thigh removed. Bit old for that now, eh?" Reggie laughed as he left the farmhouse.

Daniel stared at the closed door. Anna did have a tattoo on her inner thigh, and Reggie would only know that if they'd been intimate. "Release me, Jack, I'm going to kill him," he pleaded.

Jack put his hand on his shoulder. "And where would that leave you, Daniel? Let him go. He's out of your life now. I've got plans, Daniel. This is going to be a fresh start for you, for me, for all of us."

Jack untied Daniel and led him to the cupboard under the stairs in the hallway. "I'll show you what you came to steal," he said, pulling a key from his trouser pocket. Daniel started sweating, suddenly worried he was about to be locked in a cupboard, never to be found. He hung back.

"Don't be afraid," Jack reassured him, flicking a switch and lighting up the cupboard to reveal the contents of the small space.

Daniel froze and glanced questioningly at Jack when he saw two paintings by Edvard Munch, 'The Scream' and 'Moonlight'.

Jack pulled them out so Daniel could get a better look at them. They were exquisite. Daniel eyed them hungrily, mesmerised by their beauty.

"You're a bit of an artist yourself, are you not?" Jack asked.

"How do you know that?" Daniel said, still staring at the paintings.

"It came back to me, after that whole incident, the village house killings, your inquiry, your discharge," Jack replied. "You left behind your artwork. It became quite the talking point in the officers' mess for some time afterwards. You really have a special talent – which brings me to the next thing that's going to happen and the part you are going to play."

Daniel's heart sank. All he had wanted to do was get out of here, and it felt as though he was in a never-ending nightmare.

Having been told the part he was about to play, Daniel knew he had to let Anna and the kids go. He wasn't sure he wanted to see Anna again anyway. If what Reggie had said was true, it was the final nail in the coffin for their marriage. And Daniel knew he was about to embark on a very different life, the consequences of which Daniel did not want to affect his family. With a heavy heart, he headed home for the last time.

Part 2

Chapter 1

Anna

Settling down at Susan's house, Anna felt heartbroken, bruised and shattered. Over a few wines the night before, she had confided in her friend what had happened after she left the bar with the handsome stranger. Susan was shocked and told Anna she had to go to the police.

"There might still be evidence," Susan insisted, "you have to go to the police, Anna, it will prove to Daniel what happened to you."

"He doesn't know and I don't want him to know!" Anna cried, her face pale. "He can never find out, Susan. If he does, that will be the end of us forever, and I'm not sure I can live without him."

"So you are just going to let that piece of shit get away with it? What if he does it to some other girl?" Susan did not understand Anna's reluctance to go to the police, but she could see how fragile her friend was, so decided not to push it, for now.

Chapter 2

Daniel

With a heavy heart, Daniel returned home. The house was still empty. Anna was at Susan's with the girls, and he was glad. He didn't want to see her right now, as Reggie's words resonated over and over in his head. He felt sick at the thought of them together. He thought back to that Saturday night when Anna had been out with the girls, and how the next day she was unnaturally quiet. He'd been too distracted to really care very much but now he wished he'd been more in tune with what was going on with her.

Daniel decided to leave a note rather than contact her by phone. It was brief and to the point, and told her he was leaving for a while and that he wouldn't be contactable. He wrote that he would contact her when he could and asked her to give his love to the girls. He told her to tell them he had to go away for work, and that they were always on his mind. He finished the note with the most painful part, telling her that he knew she had been with another man and that perhaps it was time to think about divorce proceedings. He just wrote that to freak Anna out; there was no way he was going to have time to initiate a divorce right now, he had far too much on his plate. Gathering a few things together, he locked up the house and returned to Jack's farmhouse.

Chapter 3

Daniel & Jack

Jack was waiting for him and welcomed him in. "Great, you're back; now we can talk business."

"Can we eat first?" Daniel asked, suddenly realising he had not eaten for 24 hours.

"Sure," said Jack, busying himself in the kitchen. He put on a fresh pot of coffee, pulled out some ham, tomatoes and a loaf, which he cut into thick slices. Daniel's mouth drooled as he watched him. Once he was satisfied, he turned to Jack.

"Okay, so what is it exactly that you want me to do?"

Jack had begun clearing away the plates. He brought a bottle of bourbon to the table, with two glasses. "You might want a drink while I tell you," he said, pouring out two good measures. "After I came out of the army, a pal of mine, like you, was a fantastic artist; together we came up with a scheme. He would produce copies of paintings by Picasso and Lowry, two easily copied artists, and I would sell them – then we'd split the proceeds. However, my pal, I can't name any names you understand, had a sudden lack of confidence. He realised just how much money we stood to make. These paintings in the cupboard under my stairs, you think they're the real deal?" Daniel nodded, taking another sip of the bourbon. "Nope, handy work of my pal, a freaking genius. He did not have confidence in his own abilities and no amount of persuading could sway him – which leads me to you. When I saw your work back in Afghanistan, I was sorry we had not been acquainted because I tell you right now, you are even better than my pal, and what we stand to make is outrageous amounts. I don't see how you can refuse anyway, as you are in a bit of a jam now yourself."

Daniel lowered his gaze. "Yes, I am in a hell of a jam. Reggie has ruined my life, he's slept with my wife, lost me my job and dragged me to the pit of despair. I'm in a jam alright."

"Well, he's out your life now, Daniel, so I suggest you get a good night's sleep – you can take your pick from a number of spare rooms upstairs – get settled in and we'll discuss more tomorrow. I'm excited, this is going to be good for both of us, trust me."

But Daniel didn't trust him. That was the point. He hardly knew the man. Was it enough that he was at least away from his wife and his problems at home?

He chose a small room at the back of the house and unpacked his few belongings. Daniel was exhausted, and was asleep as soon as his head hit the pillow.

∞

It was the sun streaming through the thin curtains that woke him early. At first, Daniel couldn't think where he was – and then it all came back to him. Thinking about Jack, he wondered if he was a bit mad. This seemed like a crazy idea and he wasn't even sure he had the capabilities to copy such great artists' work. It was a tad exciting, though. It would give him something to take his mind off Anna. Anyway, he had hit rock bottom, and with nowhere to go from here Daniel felt he had nothing to lose.

Jack was already up and had breakfast on the go – poached eggs on toast and a pot of roasting coffee. Daniel gratefully tucked in. "So, I'm familiar with Picasso's work," said Daniel, "but this Lowry fellow not so much."

"Matchstick men and matchstick cats and dogs," sang Jack. "Sound familiar? Laurence Stephen Lowry, born 1887, died 1976. Most of his works depict Pendlebury, Lancashire, where he lived and worked. His most famous paintings were 'Going to the Match', 'Coming from the Mill' and 'Industrial Landscape', which he completed in 1955. Actually, a large collection of his works is housed at The Lowry Gallery on Salford Quays. Perhaps we should schedule a visit so you can familiarise yourself a bit better."

"Yes, that sounds like a good plan," agreed Daniel. "So, how are you going to go about selling these frauds?"

"Ah, I've got it all worked out," said Jack, a glint in his eye. "I plan to dress as a priest; I will nonchalantly visit a dealer and show him the painting. I will tell him I came across this piece at some flea market or car boot sale and ask his opinion. This is the clever bit: he will then tell me the origins and I will find out if we have managed to fool him. If he detects it's a fraud I simply laugh and say I only bought it for two quid anyway and walk away. If, however, he is fooled, I would imagine he would be excited by the find and wham bam, thank you ma'am, we have a sale. Brilliant, don't you agree?"

"Yes, that is clever," agreed Daniel. "If you are in disguise and say you picked it up at some flea market then it can never be traced back."

"Exactly," said Jack. "Don't you worry, I have it all figured out. I've been planning this for a long, long time. How fortunate you came into my life, albeit in rather negative circumstances."

Chapter 4

Anna

Anna returned to the house after dropping the girls at school and found Daniel's note. She sat with her head in her hands at the kitchen table. So he knew. She wondered how he had found out. She must try to tell him the truth and explain the man had attacked her.

Who was he anyway? He knew Daniel; Daniel must know who he was. That must be how he knew what had happened. Desperate to speak to him but with no contact number and address all she could do was wait until he rang her.

She began to change the bed sheets and get the house ready for them to move back in. There was no point staying at Susan's if Daniel wasn't even here. An hour or so later, the phone rang. Almost falling downstairs in her rush to answer the phone, Anna's heart hammered in her chest. "Hello?" she said breathlessly into the receiver.

"Anna, it's me," said Daniel. "Look, I know what you did. You've torn my heart out and stamped all over it."

"Daniel, please listen," she whispered desperately. "That night, I was out with the girls, this stranger paid me attention, flirted with me, we weren't getting on, you were drinking, you had shut yourself off from me. Anyway, I was flattered – but when we got outside, Daniel, this man attacked me down an alley!

He said it had to happen because he knew you were my husband. Who was it, Daniel?"

"So you willingly went down an alley with a total stranger?" Daniel mocked, hurt in his voice. "You expect me to believe you, when you were so flattered by a bit of attention from a stranger? You had no idea who he was and how much he wanted to hurt me and you let him. I can't do this right now; I need to go."

Before Anna could say anything, Daniel had hung up. She held the receiver close to her chest and sobbed. She had to find a way to convince him of the truth. Before she could change her mind she dialled the police and reported the attack. She was asked to come into the station and bring the clothes she was wearing that night. Thankfully, they had not been washed yet as she had been in such a rush to get out and go to Susan's. She rang Susan to see if she was free to go with her to the police station. Relieved that she was finally reporting the attack, Susan agreed.

∞

At the station, Anna was met by a sympathetic female police officer, who led her into a small office. The bag of clothes was given to another officer who took it to be analysed for DNA. Anna was asked to explain what had happened and she gave as much detail as she could. After revealing what had happened, the officer and Susan accompanied her to the hospital for a thorough medical examination. Even though it had been four days since the attack, there was the possibility that evidence might be found. There was faint bruising on both inner thighs, which was photographed as evidence and given to the police. Anna would have to wait a week before the swab test would reveal any DNA evidence.

"Why did you not report this sooner?" asked the officer gently. "There would have been a greater chance of DNA evidence."

Anna looked down at her hands. She felt worn out and fragile. "I didn't want my husband to know," she said sadly.

"What changed?" asked the officer.

"He found out. It would seem the attacker knows my husband and wanted revenge on him for some reason."

"Interesting," said the officer, thoughtfully. "Would your husband be able to come to the station for a chat at some point? Maybe he could clear up a few things and, more importantly, give us a name."

"We are estranged at the moment," Anna admitted. "I have no contact number or address. I have to wait until he contacts me before I can ask him, I'm afraid, and after the last conversation we had, God knows when that will be."

"Have you any idea at all where he could be?" asked the officer.

"None whatsoever," Anna replied. "All I can do is ask him to come into the station when he next gets in touch."

"Okay," said the officer. "Hopefully that will be sooner rather than later. We'll be in touch when the DNA results come through. If you can think of anything else at all in the meantime, call me." The officer handed Anna a card with her personal contact details on, then showed Susan and Anna to the door. "And well done for coming forward," she added. "Not many people do. It's brave and takes courage."

Anna gave a sad smile but thanked the officer before getting into Susan's car. She was emotionally drained.

Once back at the house, Susan made them both strong coffee. "Have you no idea at all where Daniel is?" she asked again, perplexed.

"No," answered Anna. "He left me a note saying he was going away for a while and would not be contactable. He said he would contact me. I have no idea where he is or what he's up to. He called me this morning and I told him what happened. He would not believe me which is why I decided to go to the police to prove to him I am telling the truth."

"Well, hopefully he will ring again soon," said Susan, putting her arm around Anna and giving her a warm hug. "He needs to tell the police who this man is so they can put him behind bars, where he belongs."

Chapter 5

Daniel

Daniel was shaking with anger after coming off the phone to Anna. How could she have been so stupid? He hated Reggie and wished he'd killed him when he had the chance.

Thinking about what Anna had said, though, she probably was telling the truth. This was something Reggie was capable of. Daniel softened as he thought about how this must be affecting Anna. He was ashamed he'd been so harsh – but then again, she had let him take her down an alley. What did she expect?

Angry again, Daniel put Anna and Reggie to the back of his mind and made his way to Jack's workshop, where an easel and art supplies awaited him. He began to doodle, practising some of Picasso's famous works. He was so immersed in what he was doing, all thoughts of Anna soon left his mind.

After several hours, Jack joined him in the workshop. He gave a low whistle. "Wow, you are better than I ever imagined," he said admiringly.

"Well, there's a long way to go yet," Daniel replied, pleased that Jack was impressed. "But I'll get there."

"I thought we might visit the Lowry gallery tomorrow morning after breakfast," Jack told him. "I think we should wear disguises. It wouldn't be the first time a fraudster was caught because he'd been filmed on CCTV casing the works of their chosen subjects."

"Oh my God, I would never have thought of that," said Daniel. "You really do have it all worked out."

Standing back to consider his artwork for the first time, Daniel thought that perhaps they could actually pull this off. He had to admit, the idea excited him; he felt alive for the first time in a long time.

The next morning, they set off in Jack's car to Manchester. It would take just over an hour and a half to get there. When they arrived at Salford Quay they had no trouble parking and were surprised at how impressive the building was, standing proudly on the quay. They were delighted to find there was a twenty-minute tour of Lowry's works and a short video of the artist, talking about his art and where he found his ideas. Daniel loved Lowry's work and thought immediately that he would have no trouble mimicking the artist. He felt a burst of excitement at the prospect and could not wait to get back to the workshop and start practising. Lowry essentially used only five colours in his artwork: flake white, ivory black, scarlet vermilion, Prussian blue and yellow ochre, all still available from the original makers, Windsor & Newton. As Lowry said himself, he was a simple man using simple materials.

∞

Back at the workshop Daniel began experimenting with

the first of his many Lowry copies. He used the flake white to cover the background, and then began working on the buildings depicted in many of his paintings. Daniel then added the people, quirky and some quite grotesque characters. There were always dogs in Lowry's work though they were somewhat cat-like in appearance.

Standing back to look at his work, Daniel was more than pleased with it. He began working more seriously on the art that Jack would take to the dealers.

After a couple of weeks, Daniel was confident enough with two paintings for Jack to take to the dealers. Jack had frames for them both. On the back of one painting he wrote 'X02030' and on the other 'X02031'. When Daniel asked why, he said, "Because it gives more authenticity and the way they are numbered may coincide with how they would have hung in the same gallery at some point."

"Ah, clever," said Daniel, "I would never have thought of that."

"Because we have no paper trail, or provenance, as they call it, this may be a problem. By adding the numbers on the backs of the paintings, it might just convince a dealer that they are the real deal," Jack explained.

Jack got changed into his priest outfit and gold-rimmed glasses. When Daniel saw him he burst out laughing, "Oh my," he exclaimed, “you really do look the part.”

“Well, who better to trust than a man of God?” asked Jack, straightening his appearance in the full-length mirror.

“Of course,” said Daniel, “who else indeed? Well, good luck old man. I’ll wait with anticipation for your safe return.”

“Yes – and hopefully we will make our first profits, too,” Jack said, as he walked out the front door, the framed paintings under his arm.

Chapter 6

Anna

Anna was still waiting to hear back from the police to see if any DNA evidence had been recovered after her swab and from the clothing she had worn on the night of the attack. She was also still waiting to hear from Daniel. She busied herself sorting out bills and doing the laundry.When the telephone rang, its shrill call made her jump.

"Hello?" she answered.

"Anna, it's me."

Anna sighed with relief. "Daniel, thank goodness you called. I reported the attack to the police. They really need to see you so you can tell them who my attacker was." She spoke quickly in case he hung up again. There was complete silence.

"What exactly did you tell them?" Daniel asked, his voice steely.

"I told them what happened and that the attacker seemed to be doing it to get revenge on you. He called you a coward." Anna felt sweat beading on her brow. "I went to the police to prove to you that I was attacked, Daniel. I definitely did not consent. I want you to know how much I love you." Anna was crying softly now.

"I know, I know, it's okay, I believe you," he cajoled. "Okay so I will go to the police station and tell them what I know of this man, which isn't really very much, I'm afraid. One day I witnessed a brutal attack on a homeless man on the way to work. I didn't want to get involved so I turned a blind eye; he sought me out and threatened me – that's when I turned to drink. I was so shaken up by him and the whole incident. He said that he would seek revenge, and apparently he has. Unfortunately, you are the one he used to hurt me." Daniel sounded upset now.

"Why didn't you tell me?" asked Anna, stronger now. "I can't believe you kept this to yourself; how awful for you."

"I didn't want to admit that I did nothing to help the man," Daniel said. "He was right about me being a coward. I could have at least called the police, raised the alarm. I was so rigid in my damn routine, I didn't want to be late for work. It sounds so lame now."

"When will you go to the police?" asked Anna.

"I'll go tomorrow morning," he answered.

"Okay, that's good," said Anna. "When can I see you? The girls miss their daddy."

"I'll swing by at the weekend but I can't come home just yet Anna. I hope you understand?"

"Yes, I understand," she answered sadly. It seemed that, even with her explanation, Daniel might not believe her and still hadn't forgiven her.

Chapter 7

Daniel

Jack was not due back until the following evening. Daniel decided he would go to the police station first thing in the morning and get it over and done with. He would be careful not to mention Jack and where he was staying. He could not lead the police anywhere near Jack's or the game would be up before it got started.

The next morning, Daniel walked into the station and asked to speak to PC Sarah Harding, the officer who had first met with Anna. She was pleased to see him and hoped he would shed light on who the mystery attacker was. She was disappointed to hear Daniel's story and description of the perpetrator; she explained that it would fit the description of many homeless men on the streets, and would make finding him a very difficult job. But she admitted it would explain why the man was seeking revenge. She shuddered at the horror of it. After half an hour or so she thanked Daniel for his help and asked where she could reach him, should they need to talk again. He gave his home telephone number and address without admitting he was not staying there. PC Harding seemed happy and Daniel left the police station, relieved that it was over and done with, for now.

Chapter 8

Jack

Jack caught the train to Manchester, where he knew he could find a dealer to sell the paintings to. As he made himself comfortable on the train he felt happy. It was a shock seeing Reggie again and finding out how much he wanted revenge; it had led him to Daniel and he was glad of that. He had lost his dear wife Sylvia to cancer, which had left him empty and bereft. Life had been pretty dull since retiring from the army and now it was full of excitement. He wasn't cash strapped, by any means, but the thought of making thousands selling frauds so that he could live a life of absolute luxury was appealing. He dreamed of a beach house, maybe in Spain or Italy. Yes, Italy, he loved everything about Italy, the food, the wine, the women, the sunshine. He closed his eyes and dozed off, dreaming of the future.

When the train pulled into Manchester, Jack was feeling confident about approaching the dealers. With Daniel's paintings under his arm, he alighted the train and set off to the town centre. There was an array of art galleries along Princess Street. He entered the first one he came to, and casually had a look around at the various art works on display. There was an emphasis on contemporary artwork. The dealer eyed the parcel under Jack's arm and approached him with a smile.

"Good morning, Father, is there anything I can help you with?" The dealer was a man who looked to be in his 50s. He had thick grey hair and wore mustard cords, a wine-coloured polo neck and a moss green cardigan. His spectacles had thick black trimming, framing his clear blue, intelligent eyes.

"Oh, good morning to you," replied Jack, feigning his poshest accent. "I'm from the Society of Jesus and my superiors have sent me here to request a valuation. Our church is undergoing some renovations and these old paintings were discovered. No-one knows anything about them or how long they were there."

Jack spoke fast.

"Oh, how interesting," enthused the dealer. "Come over to my desk and we can have a closer look." The dealer led the way to the front of the shop, where he sat behind a large oak desk. Taking the first painting, the dealer carefully removed the brown paper around it and laid it in front of him. "It's clearly a Lowry, no shadow of a doubt there. Is the other one the same?" He took the other painting and uncovered it. He then took out a magnifying glass and examined each painting carefully, taking in the buildings, the people, the dogs, then looking more closely at the signature at the very bottom of each painting. "Yes, there it is, see, signed LS Lowry. Are you familiar with his works, Father?"

"No, not at all," Jack answered. "I have to admit, I don't

know the first thing about art." Jack adopted what he felt was a clueless expression.

"Well, Lowry's work is very famous indeed," explained the dealer. "He is known for paintings of the industrial kind, as depicted in these pieces. He lived and worked in Salford for over forty years and is famous for paintings such as 'Going to Work', 'Coming from the Mill' and 'Market Scene', among others. This one is 'Going to the Match'," he informed Jack, pointing at the first of the paintings. "This one is 'Group of People'. Wonderful, really. Look at the detail in the first painting, quite incredible." The dealer was clearly impressed. Jack did a good job feigning interest in all that the dealer was telling him about Lowry. "I don't suppose you have any paperwork regarding the sale and purchase of these paintings, do you Father?"

"No, there was no paperwork found with the paintings," Jack explained. "Is it important to have documents of sale and purchase?"

"Well, yes, you see evidence is generally needed to authenticate the paintings, make sure they are the real deal. There have been many cases of fraud when it comes to Lowry's work, I'm afraid. To the naked eye I would say these are the real deal. Lowry only ever used five colours, you see, and I can see that the five used in these paintings coincides with Lowry's works."

Turning over the paintings, the dealer examined the backs.

"Well now," he said happily. "You see those numbers on the back?" He pointed out the numbers to Jack.

"Yes. Yes, what do those mean?" asked Jack, screwing up his face in faux consternation.

"Well, this may mean these two have hung together in a gallery at some point – see how the numbers are consecutive? This is very fortunate," the dealer beamed at a delighted Jack, who had heard exactly what he was hoping to hear. "Seeing this, I would be happy to make you an offer for these pieces – that's if they are for sale?" The dealer looked at Jack expectantly.

"Oh, really," exclaimed Jack, "well now, we never imagined for one minute anyone would want to buy them." The lie was natural. "We were really just interested in the origins of them and Father McNally was keen to keep them if no-one else wanted them. He has a host of artwork in his room."

"These need to be on display in a gallery," said the dealer, apparently horrified at the thought of them hung up in some fusty old bedroom. "We ourselves hold more contemporary art but I know exactly who would be interested in housing these, and that is where they should be. Trust me, Father," pleaded the dealer.

"Well now, I don't know, Father McNally will be awfully disappointed," Jack continued the facade.

"What if I give you two of my paintings along with payment for these? You can give them to Father McNally instead?" The dealer was clearly hell bent on purchasing the frauds now.

"Oh, I'm not sure," said Jack. "Can I have a look at them and I'll see if they'd be something he'd like?"

The dealer rushed from behind his desk and entered a room at the back of the gallery; he returned with two paintings, one of a beautiful country garden, and the other a portrait of a young boy with his arm around a huge dog. Both were pleasant enough.

"Wow, I think he would like those ones much better," beamed Jack. "They are so much brighter and not as depressing as those Lowry ones. I mean, some of the people in his work look a bit grotesque, if you don't mind my saying."

"Indeed they are," agreed the dealer. "Now, how about I give you £20,000 for both paintings?"

"£20,000?!" Jack exclaimed. "Oh my goodness, are you being serious now?"

"Very serious," confirmed the dealer, and Jack knew that he knew he would get a lot more for them at auction.

"Oh come on now," said Jack. "This is fantastic. You have no idea what the money could do for all the charitable organisations we are involved with. I can't believe this, I really can't." The dealer opened a drawer and pulled out a cheque book.

"Can you leave the payee unnamed for now? We'll need to

discuss how best to put the money to good use," asked Jack.

"Yes, no problem," replied the dealer, scribbling the amount and his signature. "Tell you what, I'll leave the date blank, too, in case it takes you a while." And he laughed.

Chapter 9

Daniel & Jack

Back at the farmhouse, Daniel waited nervously for Jack to return. Could they actually pull this off? He was worried that Jack had been caught and was being held at some police station. They hadn't discussed what they would say or do in that event. Would Jack report him? He wasn't sure, it wasn't as though he owed him anything. On the contrary, he had tried to rob him, and they weren't exactly friends. Daniel made a mental note to discuss being caught when Jack got back; he had to know if his back was covered. He boiled the kettle and made the twentieth cup of tea that day.

Just then, he heard Jack's car approaching and quickly made him a cup, too. "Well?" he said as Jack entered the house. "How did it go?"

Jack's face looked sombre. He shook his head slowly, and Daniel felt disappointment well up inside him.

Unable to keep up the facade Jack burst out laughing and brandished the cheque in front of his face. "Twenty grand!" he confirmed. "Ten grand each and that's just the start of things."

"How much?" cried Daniel, relieved. "Bloody hell, I can't believe you pulled it off. Tell me everything." Jack told Daniel the whole story. They laughed at the bit about Father McNally wanting to keep the paintings. Daniel thought that was a stroke of genius and showed how naive the priest was about the paintings' value – had they been real ones, of course. Jack said he thought he could have got more for them, and that the dealer most certainly would, but how could he have sought more, when he was playing the part of a novice?

Daniel was delighted the paintings had sold for that much. He had not expected them to. He thought the dealer would have guessed they were fakes right away and, at best, Jack would have returned home with them. They laughed again at the two extra paintings they had acquired for the fictional priest and agreed they were probably not worth a lot of money.

Jack told him about the dealer saying how many times Lowry's works had been copied, and that if it hadn't been for the numbers on the back he doubted he would have been able to sell them at all. "Maybe we should concentrate on another artist," said Jack, thoughtfully. "One that hasn't been so widely copied and one whose work sells for a great deal of money."

Daniel was gutted, after all the hard work he'd put into copying Lowry, but he could see the wisdom in what Jack said. There was no point continuing if there was a bigger chance they would be caught on account of there being many copies of his works. "Have you got anyone in mind?" he asked.

"Are you any good at painting horses?" Jack shot back.

Chapter 10

Anna

Anna had heard back from the police. DNA was found on the clothes she had provided. There was no match on the database. With the lack of evidence, along with Daniel's description of the homeless man, it left them with not a lot to go on. They suggested Anna would benefit from counselling. She dismissed this idea. She was more worried about the state of her marriage and had pushed all thoughts of that hideous night to the darkest recess of her mind.

Busy with the children, the house and her hairdressing, Anna was getting on with her life. She hated to admit that she was enjoying life without Daniel's tight schedules: life was easier, tea was when they were hungry, not the same time every night. The girls seemed happier, and the atmosphere in the house was lighter. Anna found that they were not missing Daniel one bit.

Chapter 11

Daniel

"Alfred Munnings," said Jack. "Not exactly obscure; once one of the giants of the 20th century. He loved to paint the English countryside, a naturalist, he was a hater of modern art and was very vocal about it, too. During the First World War he was deemed unfit for service due to an eye injury but was employed by the army to prepare horses for war. Later, he was employed as a war artist and is famous for many pictures depicting soldiers on horseback going into battle. Horses were his great love and feature in a prominent number of his works. Later, he was rather infatuated with the gypsies and travellers he met while on his travels. They inspired his early works, such as the green wagon and Irish ponies in a grassy lane. He was inspired by the richness of the colours of their clothes and their wagons. He was a careful observer of nature, painting equestrian scenes, lots of colour, lots of movement with local characters and attention to detail. He mostly used water colours and oils. So that's good news for you."

Daniel was listening intently, impressed by Jack's knowledge. This artist was a very different one from Lowry, whose characters were sometimes grotesque and dark. This was a new challenge and he very much liked the sound of it.

"More importantly, can we expect to make money from copying his work?" asked Daniel.

"Oh, only six figure sums I would guess," answered Jack, smiling. "I'll get you some prints so you can get to work copying. See if you think you can pull this off. I think a trip to Essex and the Munnings Art Museum is on the cards."

The next day, Daniel got to work. Jack had provided him with prints of 'Chestnuts in Bloom' and 'A Gypsy Encampment'.

'Chestnuts in Bloom' was a picture of exactly that. The artist's use of reflection and shadowing was mind-blowing. One could almost feel the heat of the summer sun as it reflected off the greenery, making the viewer want to duck under the blooms for a bit of shade. 'A Gypsy Encampment' was a totally different piece, with people, a horse, a dog and a foreboding dark sky, and the ever-present countryside in the background. Daniel recognised the skill of the man in the people he drew. They were so in proportion and detailed; lifelike. Munnings captured the scene so well Daniel felt mimicking it would be an overwhelming challenge – but one he felt excited about.

A few days later, Daniel and Jack visited the Munnings Art Museum. Daniel was bowled over by the artist's work. The detail he put into every person and animal he painted must have been painstaking. His country scenes went on for miles and miles. He could feel the artist's love of the countryside in his paintings. It was definitely worth the visit. It gave Daniel more insight into the man, the characteristics of his works, and the scenes he loved.

As with the Lowry visit he could not wait to get back to the farmhouse and start painting more of Munnings' works. He'd need a bit more time with this artist, perfecting the fine details, but he felt confident he could do it.

A few weeks later, Jack's jaw dropped as he walked into the farmhouse to see some of Daniel's fake Munnings paintings on display. "You are an absolute talent," he murmured. "To the naked eye, that's Munnings' work right there. How do you do it?"

Jack stepped back a bit to admire the paintings.

"With a lot of hard work and a good eye for detail," Daniel replied, pleased that Jack was so enthralled by his work. "I should have two ready for you by the end of the week."

"Fantastic. I look forward to the sell. It shouldn't be hard if the last time was anything to go by." Jack continued staring at the paintings, a slight smile on his lips.

Chapter 12

Tony Capaldi

Tony was a talent. Growing up he was the talk of his household; before he knew it he was the talk of the town, then the district, then the whole country.

At the age of eight, when he woke on Christmas Day he found that Santa had been down the chimney and left him a snooker table. As he picked up the cue and placed his hand on the green baize, he thought it would be easier to get the balls in the pockets than to miss. After all, that was what the game was about. When a ball hit the back of the table's plastic pockets and sunk from view, Tony glowed with satisfaction.

All the other kids on the street would be out playing or stuck in their rooms on their computer games, but not Tony. As he grew older and got to experience the proper table, he had an almost magical control of the cue ball. He wasn't just a master of snooker; he was a master of physics. Shot after shot he commanded the cue ball to screw back, back spin, sidespin, stun… it all came rather easily to him.

Not surprisingly, Tony started to get publicity and, with it, attention – good and bad. His agent and promoters organised photo shoots and modelling campaigns, keen to make a buck out of his good looks, which would in turn promote their events and attract the sponsors that were vital for the game to survive.

Tony found that he was the star attraction and made some good money. He went to a tailor and was fitted for fabulous, well-cut suits. He was manicured, shaved and his black hair cut into the latest style. Men envied him, women wanted to be with him… and many were. He was fond of women and drink and his morals were lacking. A few years down the line, he had gained a reputation for being a ladies' man and was fast becoming an alcoholic. Still he managed to be Britain's number one snooker player.

Things took a downward spiral when the drink became a real problem. His hands would shake without a drink in them and of course this had a negative effect on his game.

People in the business began to lose faith in Tony and concentrated instead on other young, up-and-coming stars. Tony realised he was losing it and wasn't surprised when his manager suggested he take a break, book a retreat, get clean and return when he was able to hold the damn cue without shaking like a junkie.

Tony spent some time travelling around Europe. He could afford to stay in the best hotels. Eat in the finest restaurants. He met some interesting people and found he was capable of staying off the drink when he wanted to. He was walking, hiking, and swimming in lakes. It felt great to be healthy for once.

While he was sobering up, his thoughts became clearer and

as he looked back on his life he was ashamed of it. The women, the drinking, the general bad living… there had to be more to life. He had been brought up a Catholic but had veered off the religious path at an early age; he now found himself praying like he had never prayed before. He prayed to God for the strength to stay away from alcohol and women, he prayed for a more meaningful life, he promised God he would do good in his life from now on.

When Tony returned home, his manager was delighted to see the change in him. For another year, Tony continued playing snooker and making more money but he could see the younger talent coming up and he wanted to end his snooker career on a high note, having regained his reputation. His manager was disappointed; he was wealthy because of Tony's talent and he didn't want it to stop.

Tony used his money wisely and invested in several enterprises, including an art gallery in Manchester. He had developed an interest in the finer things in life and art was one of them. The profits his businesses made were spread out among several charities. Tony was giving back, just like he promised God he would, and he felt good about it.

His friend Alistair ran the art gallery and Tony would often spend time helping Alistair out and learning more about the art world. He found it fascinating. Alistair called him one morning to say he had come down with a bout of 'flu and since Tony knew a fair bit about the gallery now he wondered if Tony could help out, rather than shutting the gallery for a few days. Tony agreed – and was there the morning Jack paid a visit.

Chapter 13

Jack & Tony

"Hello Father, how can I help you?" Tony asked, looking up to see a priest enter the gallery.

"Good morning. I was looking for a valuation on some paintings," Jack replied, using again his posh accent.

"Let me guess – are you Anglican? Catholic? Episcopalian, maybe?" probed Tony.

"No, I'm from the Society of Jesus," Jack replied, feeling suddenly uncomfortable with the line of questioning. He knew he should have done more research,

"Ah, the Jesuits," continued Tony. "*Ad majorem dei gloriam…*" Tony was bowing his head but looked up at Jack as he added, "*inque hominum.*"

"*Inque hominum,*" Tony repeated, and Jack realised he was expected to respond in some way. He shifted from one foot to the other in the awkward pause. Tony bowed his head again and recited the Latin phrase in its entirety. "*Ad majorem dei gloriam inque hominum salerum.*"

Jack smiled smoothly. "But of course. Quite," he said softly.

"Hard men, the Jesuits," Tony said with a smile. "Got my utmost respect. It's an order that receives the most thorough training. The family sometimes holiday in the Basque region of

Spain. You are always in our prayers." Tony's smile widened.

"Well, thank you very much for your prayers and well wishes," Jack replied, wishing the guy would stop blabbing on. It was deeply disconcerting.

"Every July 31st, we pop along to say mass on your patron saint's day. Forgive me, Father, I've momentarily forgotten the patron's name. It's St… St Jude…" The end of Tony's sentence hung in the air.

"Yes, St Jude Thaddeus," finished Jack, grateful he had learned one thing at least.

"Yes, quite," said Tony, lowering his gaze. "Anyway, back to your original enquiry. Unfortunately, the dealer is ill and won't be back in the gallery for a few days, if you'd like to pop back then?"

Jack's disappointment was visible. "Oh. That's a pity. Okay yes, that's what I will do." Jack turned and headed for the door. He was anxious to get out of there before this guy asked him any more religious questions.

"Before you go, I have a gift for you," Tony said, heading towards the back of the shop. He returned moments later with a £50 note. "For the Jesuit missions," he said, pressing the note into Jack's hand. Jack gave a grateful smile and left the shop before the talkative man could ask him for a blessing.

∞

That night, back at his mansion, it was time for Tony's Examen. He thought about the day that had been and focused on the people he had met. He thought about them again, this time with gratitude. He meditated on the presence of God in them, and paid attention to any change in his emotions and feelings.

And Tony sat bolt upright, in a moment of pure clarity.

Wait a minute, he thought. *I gave that guy £50 for the Jesuit missions and he isn't even a priest, let alone a Jesuit one. He didn't know his own order's patron saint, never mind his own order's motto.*

Chapter 14

Jack

Jack's confidence was low as he walked away from the gallery. How could he have been so stupid as to not have carried out some research? He was well aware the guy probably knew he didn't have a clue what he was talking about, and that put him in a dangerous position. He considered what to do next. Should he take the risk and visit another dealer or go home and rethink his disguise, then try again? He knew Daniel would be waiting back at the farmhouse for good news and decided to visit one more dealer before giving up. Surely the next one wouldn't be a Catholic, too.

He walked to the next gallery and waltzed in with a cheerful "Good morning to you!" aimed at the dealer. "I'm from the Society of Jesus and my superiors sent me here to request a valuation."

Jack repeated the story about the paintings being discovered in the church during the renovations. The dealer recognised them as Munnings straight away. He was very interested in both paintings and not a flicker of doubt seemed to pass through his mind that they were not originals. He offered Jack a staggering amount. Jack almost fainted, but remained calm and said how grateful the order would be and how many charities would be helped through this sizeable donation. Again he asked that the payee be left unwritten – and he almost danced his way back to the station.

On the train home, Jack couldn't help but feel unnerved by the conversation with the guy in the first gallery. He knew he had messed up and that it would be discussed in the area. People would start putting two and two together. The cheque in his hand would make both he and Daniel rich and perhaps it was time to visit new areas or even call it a day.

He did not want to get caught, and his dreams of retiring to a pretty Italian resort go up in smoke. But it had been exciting and it was a shame to give up now. The stakes were too high.

Chapter 15

Daniel

Meanwhile, back at the farmhouse Daniel called Anna. "Hi, it's me," he said coolly. "How have you been?"

"Hi," replied Anna, and she didn't sound overly excited to hear from him either. "I'm fine," she told him.

"And the girls?" he asked. Anna sighed.

"They are fine, too," she replied tightly, and Daniel could hear her biting back what she really wanted to say.

"Have the police been back in touch?" he asked, holding his breath.

"Yes. They haven't found anything new. There was DNA but no match and, truthfully, they do not have a whole lot to go on." Anna sounded sad.

"Oh, that's frustrating," said Daniel, relieved that the heat was off. "I was thinking of coming home for the weekend." Actually, he did not relish the thought of returning; if he was being honest, he was happier on his own. He did not think he could look at Anna again without imagining what had happened with Reggie. He shuddered at the thought.

"We have plans for the weekend," said Anna quickly.

Daniel wondered if this was true but, "Oh," he said, relieved. "Okay, maybe another time?"

"Maybe," replied Anna uncertainly, and then she hung up

the phone.

After the call, Daniel sat down heavily at the kitchen table, hands on head. His marriage was over. He wasn't even sad about it; he knew he had changed. He could not return home and be the man he was. He knew this with startling clarity.

∞

Jack bustled in through the front door beaming like a Cheshire cat. "Daniel, my boy, we are rich," he said, brandishing the cheque in front of Daniel's eyes, which nearly popped out of his head when he saw how much it was for.

"Bleeding heck," he said, sitting back down before he fell down. "This is unbelievable. Tell me the whole story."

Jack told him about the visit to the first dealer and how he thought he'd been rumbled with the whole priest persona and how his confidence was shaken. Then he went on to tell him about his good fortune with the next dealer and how he had come about receiving a cheque that would make them both rich.

"I think it's time for me to hang up the old priest routine," said Jack regretfully.

"But I have another four Munnings ready for the off," said Daniel, disappointed. He had worked solidly on those, and was proud of how they had turned out.

"I know, we just have to weigh up the risks," said Jack sensibly. "One thing's for sure, I cannot portray a priest again. In fact, I'm not sure it's a good idea for me to visit any of the dealers again."

"If not you, then why not me?" suggested Daniel with a twinkle in his eye. "My marriage is over, Jack. I need to start a new life and I know this cheque would see me well for a good few years. It would be even better to sell the ones I have ready to really live out life in style."

Chapter 16

Daniel

Daniel grew a beard and moustache, something he had never done before. He kind of liked it, though. It would all be coming off as soon as he had made his sale. He found a pair of round spectacles and a flat cap and dressed in a hippy style; not him at all. His dress sense was normally much smarter.

He and Jack had decided he should try his luck in Bristol, wanting to give Manchester a miss after Jack's run-in with the Catholic dealer. Daniel was nervous as hell but he had practised what he was going to say. Laden with two of the Munnings copies, he set off. Entering the first gallery, Daniel had a good look around and spotted the dealer behind a large oak desk. He looked to be in his early thirties, intelligent looking in a nerdy way, wearing an oversized shirt and cords.

"Can I help you at all?" asked the man, smiling.

"Yes please," answered Daniel, "I wondered if you could give me a valuation on these two paintings. They were left to me. My uncle passed away twenty years ago and left them to my cousin. He passed away suddenly at the start of the year. I inherited them, being the only living relative." The dealer took the paintings from Daniel and laid them out on the desk, unwrapping them from the brown coverings. His eyes widened in surprise.

"Oh my. You have two Alfred Munnings paintings here."

His eyes scanned the artwork. “This one is ‘Gypsy Tales’, depicting a gypsy lady telling stories to two young girls, presumably her daughters.

“Alfred was infatuated with the gypsies he met on his travels. Their use of colours inspired him and he often painted gypsy scenes. The next one is ‘My Wife, My Horse’ – he has cleverly painted himself in there, do you see? He is actually holding the painting in his hands, that’s how much he loved this one. In fact, everything he held most dear are in this picture: his wife, his horse and his home.” The dealer was delighted and clearly could not believe his luck that he should have them in his possession. “Do you have any paperwork to go with the paintings?” he asked.

“Paperwork?” asked Daniel, feigning confusion. “What kind of paperwork?”

“You know, receipts, proof of purchase – your uncle would’ve had it when he bought these. Do you know where he purchased them?” the dealer probed.

“Unfortunately not,” said Daniel, lowering his eyes, “my uncle lived in Scotland and I haven’t been there since I was a child. When he died my cousin, I presume, took over the clearing and emptying of the house before selling. I was not given any paperwork with the paintings.”

“Oh, that is a pity,” said the dealer, his expression

displaying his extreme disappointment. "The days of selling paintings with a smile and a handshake are very much in the past."

"I understand," said Daniel, "I know someone else who is interested in the paintings, a dealer in London. I am not planning to visit there for some months so I thought I would try to get a valuation here first, since I am in the area."

The dealer thought for a bit. "You know, I am more than sure this is Munnings' work. I'd really hate to miss the opportunity to purchase them from you. I can offer you a good price."

Daniel pretended to mull it over and then agreed to sell them. The dealer was delighted and wrote a six figure cheque. Daniel asked him to leave the payee blank as he wanted to donate the money to brain cancer research in his cousin's name, and he wasn't yet sure who he should make the cheque payable to.

"How very generous of you," the dealer gushed.

"Trust me, I don't need the money," Daniel told him, "I am just glad the paintings are with someone who appreciates them so much and the money will be donated to such a worthwhile cause." They shook hands and Daniel left the shop.

Full of confidence now, Daniel could not wait to sell his last two Munnings. He talked it over with Jack and they decided he should take them to London, figuring that was where he would make the most money. He kept his disguise and took the train to

London the next day. This was going to be his final sale and he wanted it to be a good one. Daniel and Jack already had plenty of money; this final sale would ensure a lifetime of luxury. He also wanted to give Anna and the girls enough cash so they would never have to worry about money again. He knew the marriage was over but he still cared for Anna and especially his girls. Once he was settled in his new life he was planning to arrange custody so he could have the girls every other weekend and keep them in his life.

Daniel arrived in London and made his way to the city centre. He stopped for lunch before visiting several galleries. Looking at a vast array of paintings in one, he had the two remaining Munnings copies under his arm. He was standing looking in awe at Van Gogh's 'A Starry Night', the Don McLean song playing over in his head – "I could have told you Vincent, this world was never made for one as beautiful as you."

Lost in thought, he did not hear footsteps approaching. A hand laid on his shoulder made him jump and when he turned to see who it was his jaw dropped.

"Reggie!"

"Hello, Daniel," said Reggie, smoothly. He was clean shaven and wore a black turtleneck and camel coat, Crombie style, with black jeans and brown brogues. He looked handsome and healthy.

"Reggie, what are you doing here?" Daniel asked, trying to hide his shock.

"I moved here," he answered. "I saw you eating lunch earlier. At first I didn't believe it was you. I followed you and then I knew it was you by the way you walk, the way you carry yourself. What have you got, Daniel?" he asked, looking pointedly at the parcel under Daniel's arm.

Daniel looked down and he knew that Reggie would know what he was up to. Why did he choose to come to London? Reggie was the last person he wanted or expected to see. It was too much of a coincidence.

"None of your bloody business," he spat back, all pleasantries gone. "Go back to the hole you came from."

"Ouch, that's not very nice," replied Reggie, feigning hurt. "I could call you out right now. Right this minute. Will I call over the dealer to take a very good look at these paintings?"

"Don't you bloody dare," said Daniel, pushing past him. "Get out of my way and out of my life." He carried on walking and was relieved not to hear Reggie's footsteps behind him. Once outside the gallery he ducked into an alleyway and kept an eye on the door of the gallery. When he saw Reggie leave he followed him, making sure he was unseen.

Daniel followed Reggie for several blocks, his mind running wildly. He would not allow this poor excuse for a human being to ruin his life any more. He had to do something to make sure of that – and he saw his chance as Reggie waited on the kerb to cross the busy London street. Without thinking, Daniel gave him an almighty shove, using the weight of the paintings. The brown paper concealing them ripped away with the contact, and Reggie plunged into the road.

Daniel felt a momentary horror as Reggie was crushed under the wheels of a bus full of shocked looking passengers. He hurried away into the crowds and did not stop running until he could run no more.

Chapter 17

Daniel & Jack

Back at the farmhouse, Daniel relayed the story to a horrified Jack. "Bloody hell," said Jack, reaching for the bourbon and two glasses. "Did anyone see you push him?"

"Not that I'm aware of," replied Daniel, visibly shaken. "It all happened so fast. One minute he was standing there… I had to take the opportunity. I had no choice," he added looking down at his feet.

"I understand," said Jack. "You had no choice, he would never have left you alone and you did the right thing." Both men drank back the bourbon in silence. Both were shocked by Reggie's death and Daniel's part in it. "I think it's time I made my plans for my new life abroad," announced Jack. "We've plenty of money now, Daniel, I'm happy with what I've got."

Daniel remained silent; he wasn't planning on giving up selling the two remaining Munnings copies. He would sell them himself before embarking on his new life.

The next day, Daniel packed up his belongings and said farewell to Jack. The two had grown close and he was sorry that this would probably be the last time he saw Jack. He had hired a car and rented a flat in Yorkshire on a short-term lease. He didn't plan to be there long – just enough to sell the paintings, see Anna and the girls alright and then start a new life elsewhere. The flat was basic but fine for his needs for now. He had called Anna and was going to visit tonight to chat things over. He did not relish the thought of seeing her but knew he could not put it off any more.

∞

"Dad!" Eloise answered the door. At ten she had grown up so much since the last time he saw her. He opened his arms for a hug, but Eloise seemed reluctant to step into them – until she did, and then she gave him a tight squeeze. "Mum, Dad's here!" she shouted, eager for someone else to join them. Anna came out the kitchen looking flustered.

"Daniel, hi," she said, not smiling. "Come through."

Daniel entered the house, feeling like a stranger in his own home. It looked nice, warm, inviting. He could see the changes Anna had made to the place. It looked a lot more feminine; well, after all it was only girls living here.

"The place looks nice," he said.

"Thanks," Anna answered, looking a little guilty at the changes she had made without consulting him. "I didn't think you'd mind," she added, "since you're never here."

"No, no of course not," he said, sitting down at the kitchen table. "How have you been?"

"Good, yeah, fine, busy, you know, with the girls, work, that kind of thing," she said as she made them a coffee.

"I thought it was time we had a talk about the future," said

Daniel. “Do you want me to come home?”

Anna dropped a spoon, startled by his sudden question. Slowly picking up the spoon again, she looked at him. She could see he could still not look at her, not properly anyway. “Would you want to?” she asked, holding her breath.

He was silent, thinking it through. “No, not really, if I’m being totally honest. This time we have been apart, I’ve changed, Anna,” and he looked at her for the first time. “I mean, really changed. I’m not the same man, I don’t think it would work.”

Letting out a sigh of relief, Anna laughed nervously. “I’ve changed too, Daniel. I’m not the same woman since the attack…” her voice trailed off. “Anyway, the girls and I have gotten used to you not being here and we’re actually getting on fine, we’re happy.”

Daniel was only partly relieved. He hadn’t expected this to be easy but Anna’s apparent lack of need for him was slightly painful.

“I’m thinking of going to Canada for a bit,” said Daniel. “There’s an art college I’d like to go to. The course is for two years.”

“Two years?” said Anna. “That’s a long time in the girls’ life, Daniel.”

“Yes I know, I was hoping they could come out and visit me there,” he said.

"That would be a hell of an expense," remarked Anna.

"Money's not a problem," he told her, pulling out the cheque from the Bristol dealer. He had written Anna's name as the payee. Anna took in a large breath when she saw how much the cheque was for.

"What? How?" she exclaimed, looking from the cheque to Daniel and back again.

"Best not to ask questions," he explained. "I sold my art, the dealer loved it and I'm just as shocked as you that he gave me that much."

"No way," said Anna. "A new artist on the scene would never have made this much. What's the truth, Daniel?"

"The truth is I sold art," he said sternly. "That's all you need to know. Now take this money and use it wisely for you and the girls. Once I'm set up in Canada I will be in touch and you and the girls can come over for a visit. If you don't want to, just send the girls. I want to be in their lives, Anna."

She was too overwhelmed to question him any more about the cheque and put it away in her bag without saying another word.

Chapter 18

Daniel

Daniel settled well in Canada. He loved the art course he signed up for and made some interesting friends along the way. He rented a house with a stunning garden, overlooking a gorgeous blue lake. The house was fully furnished, which had not come cheap, but he could afford it. He had successfully sold the two remaining paintings and was satisfied he had enough money to live out the rest of his life in comfort.

Daniel met a girl, Grace; she was every bit as beautiful as her name. She had long golden hair, bright blue eyes and her bright and bubbly personality was a breath of fresh air. She was stunning and Daniel could not believe his luck in finding her. He had never imagined for a minute that he would ever get romantically involved with anyone again after Anna but it had just happened. Grace was easy going and fun to be around. She was an artist, too; they had met at college. She couldn't believe Daniel was there at all because he was so talented.

"You don't need tuition," she had said but he said he could always learn something new and, anyway, he enjoyed it.

Having somewhere to go every day, and meeting new people, they soon fell into an easy pace of life. Grace ended up moving in with him to save her paying for accommodation. He felt guilty when he thought about Anna but he was so far away from home, it was easy to forget his past and all the horrors that went with it.

Chapter 19

DI Sarah Harding

Back in Yorkshire, Detective Inspector Sarah Harding was looking at a new case that had landed on her desk. It was the case of a man who had died after been pushed in front of a London bus. A witness had come forward and claimed he saw a man, carrying what seemed to be paintings under his arm, push the victim into the path of the bus. The case had been transferred to all units after London police had come up with no leads. Sarah studied the face of the victim. Something in the back of her mind clicked; she recognised this face from a description she had been given. Who by?

She closed her eyes and thought hard. A million different cases came to her mind – then she remembered, very clearly. Before Sarah's promotion, Anna Edgar had given a description of the man who attacked her, and it matched the image of the man Sarah was staring at right now.

It didn't seem possible but her instincts kicked in and something in her mind told her that this was the same man. A DNA match from the victim to the clothes provided by Anna confirmed her suspicions.

The next day, she arrived at Anna's door. Once inside, she showed Anna a picture of the man. Anna winced in shock. He was in a bad way but his facial features were still clear.

"That's him," Anna said, white as sheet. "That's the man who attacked me. What happened to him?"

"Yes, indeed, a DNA match confirmed this. He was hit by a bus in London," said Sarah. "Actually, he was pushed in front of it. A witness said he saw a man with what he thinks were paintings under his arm push him in front of the bus."

Anna sat down quickly. She put her head in her hands and tried to breathe normally. She knew in an instant it was Daniel. It must have been Daniel. She felt her stomach suddenly heave and ran to the toilet to throw up.

When she returned to the kitchen, the DI was looking sympathetic. "I can't say I'm sorry he's dead," Anna admitted.

"No, I daresay you're not, after what he did to you," said Sarah. "Nevertheless, it is now a murder investigation and despite who he is and what he has done, a thorough investigation will take place. Is your husband around?" Sarah glanced round the room but could see no signs a man might be living there.

"No," answered Anna quickly. "We're actually separated. We hadn't been getting on for a while, and then after the attack, it was just impossible."

"That's a shame," said Sarah, "Do you know where I can get in touch with Daniel?"

"I believe he's no longer in the country," said Anna

vaguely. She knew Daniel was in trouble and she didn't want to tell the police where he was.

"Oh. So where is he?" probed Sarah. "I presume he would want to keep in contact with the children, if not you?"

"He contacts us," Anna lied. "He said he would let me know details of where he is when he settles somewhere."

"Well, next time he gets in touch, find out exactly where he is," Sarah instructed. "It's vitally important we contact him."

"You don't think he's involved do you?" Anna asked, looking horrified at the idea.

"It's more to rule him out of our enquiries," said Sarah smoothly. "After all, the victim was fixated on getting revenge on your husband; a fact that cannot be ignored and needs further investigation."

Sarah stood up to leave, and Anna felt an enormous sense of relief. She needed time alone to process what had just happened – and she had to contact Daniel to warn him.

As Sarah drove away, she thought about her next move. Paintings – the suspect was carrying paintings. She would pay a visit to some art galleries in the area where Reggie was killed and see if the suspect had visited any; there should be some CCTV.

Sarah struck gold at the first gallery she visited. It kept a month's worth of CCTV footage and, sitting in a small office, she carefully scanned images from the day of Reggie's death.

Nothing in the morning showed anything of interest. She was beginning to think she would not find anything; then early afternoon showed a man entering the gallery carrying a painting-shaped parcel under his arm.

Sarah's heart began pounding. She could not believe her eyes. It looked like Daniel Edgar; though he had a beard, moustache and flat cap hiding his hair, he had the same build and gait as Daniel. She followed with her eyes as he moved around the gallery, stopping to admire Van Gogh's work; and then another man entering the screen, well dressed, handsome, dark hair. It was undeniably Reggie.

Reggie laid his hand on Daniel's shoulder and the two men engaged in conversation. Since there was no sound, Sarah couldn't hear what was being said. Perhaps a lip reader would be able to work it out, she thought. The conversation looked as though it was getting heated, and ended with Daniel pushing past Reggie and leaving the gallery. Reggie looked after Daniel with a smirk on his face, changing his handsome features to ones of menace. He left soon after.

Sarah took the video evidence away with her. She walked along the street to the road where Reggie was killed.

Standing at the road he had been about to cross, she scanned the streets above, looking for CCTV in the area. She saw several cameras above shops and visited each to see if there was any evidence of Daniel and Reggie. The shopkeepers told her that the London police had already taken the videos of that particular day.

Sarah went to London headquarters to speak to the officer in charge of the case, to see if he would share with her any findings. She was dismayed to find that the footage they did have was so grainy it was impossible to make out who was who in any of them.

"What's the point of having CCTV if it's so useless?" she asked the officer in frustration.

"I know, it's pointless," he agreed. "They just don't want to spend the money on more sophisticated equipment, not realising what they have is virtually useless." He was just as disappointed. Sarah shared with him the video she had retrieved from the gallery. He was impressed and surprised that she thought she knew not only who the victim was, but also who the other man was with the paintings. She told him of the attack report and all that she knew about Anna and Daniel Edgar. He listened in fascination.

"Do you believe she really does not know the whereabouts of her husband?" he asked when Sarah was finished.

"I'm not sure," she replied. "When she first reported the attack, she was not in contact with him, so it's possible she is telling the truth."

"Get her phone tapped and her phone records," said the officer. "He has to be found and fast."

Chapter 20

Daniel

Daniel was napping on the couch when the phone rang. He slowly stood up to answer it. "Hey," he said lazily.

"Daniel, it's me," said Anna urgently. He could tell by her voice something was very wrong.

"Anna," he replied. "What's up?"

"The police have been here, Daniel. I know Reggie is dead," she answered shakily. There was a moment's silence. Daniel felt suddenly lightheaded and sat down.

"What? How?"

"I think you know, Daniel. There was a witness who saw a man carrying two paintings, who pushed him in front of that bus." Daniel could hardly breathe, now he knew he'd been caught.

"Did you tell the police where I was?" he asked.

"No," Anna replied, "I lied because somehow I know you did this, Daniel." Silence again.

"Don't tell them where I am, Anna," he pleaded.

"They will find out eventually," she said. "It's only a matter of time and they will probably find out I lied." She was crying now.

"Don't worry, they won't unless you tell them," he consoled her. "I need to go now. I may not be in touch for a while. I will when I feel it's safe to do so."

"Daniel, I understand why you did it," Anna said quietly. "I'm not sorry he's dead." Daniel did not reply but instead softly put down the receiver. He had to get away from here – to where, he had no idea.

He packed up his belongings and left a note for Grace saying he had to return to Yorkshire on urgent business and that he did not know when or if he would return. He was sad; for the first time in a while he had been happy and he really liked Grace but he knew he could not stay here. Leaving Grace behind was kindest in the long run. He could not risk getting her caught up in this.

He paid a visit to a seedy part of town and found a man who would forge passports and documents for a fee. He changed his name to Steven Arnold and made his way to the airport. Once there he bought a one-way ticket to Italy – he was going to find Jack.

He remembered conversations with Jack about Italy and he knew Jack wanted to visit Palermo, in Sicily. He had mentioned visiting a cathedral there but essentially he had his heart set on retiring to a beach resort; he thought he may have settled at a beach resort near Palermo.

Mondello Beach was the obvious choice and Daniel knew the beauty of the white beaches and blue sea would be enough to seduce Jack.

Chapter 21

Sarah Harding

Sarah returned to Anna's house and asked for her most recent telephone records. She placed a tap on the handset. "Still not heard from him?" she asked Anna. Lowering her eyes, Anna shook her head, unconvincingly. Sarah looked at her with something like understanding in her eyes; after all, Anna had loved her husband. He had killed the man who attacked her. She wasn't going to tell them where he was. But they would find out.

Back at the station, Sarah began scrutinising the phone records. A Canadian number stood out and when she rang it a woman answered.

"Can I speak to Daniel Edgar please?" Sarah asked.

"I'm sorry, he is not here," replied the woman.

"This is Detective Inspector Sarah Harding, of West Yorkshire Police. Who am I speaking with?" Sarah asked.

"My name is Grace," the woman replied.

"Are you a friend of Daniel's?" Sarah continued to question.

"Yes, you could say that," Grace replied. "I am, was, his girlfriend. Daniel and I were studying art together here. We were living together – until I came home to find a note saying he had returned to Yorkshire on urgent business and may not be coming back." At this Grace got upset.

"Do you have any idea at all where he might have gone?" asked Sarah.

"No," replied Grace, shortly.

"What day did you say you found the note?" asked Sarah, grabbing a pen.

"Thursday, last week," Grace answered. The same day Sarah had visited Anna and told her of the witness to Reggie's death. A coincidence? Sarah thought not. Anna had tipped him off. She ended the conversation with Grace. She knew it was going nowhere and that Grace definitely did not know of Daniel's whereabouts. She didn't think he would be so stupid to return to Yorkshire. He could be anywhere in the world. The only way Sarah could investigate further would be to visit Canada to see if there were any clues there. She also knew her superiors would never agree to it. They'd say it was too expensive and a wild goose chase – she could hear it now. No, her only chance was if Daniel contacted Anna again – and she really doubted he would. The man was far too clever to fall into that trap. She planned to visit Anna again and try to appeal to her sense of duty, to try and trap Daniel; but she knew it would probably come to nothing.

Chapter 22

Anna

Anna knew the police suspected she knew of Daniel's whereabouts and was very nervous when they took away the telephone records. They would discover the number in Canada. Hopefully Daniel would be long gone and she had no clue where he was now. She grabbed her coat. Susan had called her and asked her round for lunch. It would be good to have someone to chat with about all her fears. Having told Susan everything already, she trusted her implicitly.

"Come in," said Susan, scanning the streets outside her doorway. She looked anxious.

"What's going on?" asked Anna, also having a quick scan of the streets. Had she been followed here? She didn't think so. Once inside the kitchen and seated at the kitchen table, Susan quietly told her that Daniel had called. He was in Italy and was hoping to settle there for a while. He had not dared call Anna and wanted Susan to relay a message. He told Susan he was missing his wife and family and once settled he wanted them to pack up and come to live with him. Anna was in a state of shock; this was a huge turnaround. As far as she was concerned, the marriage was over.

"What are you thinking?" asked Susan.

"I'm thinking I thought we were happier apart," replied

Anna honestly. “The girls do miss their father but I don’t know, Susan, a new life in Italy, it’s a bit extreme. I feel I’ve got some serious thinking to do.”

Susan made them some lunch while Anna told her of her fears that the police knew she was lying about Daniel’s whereabouts, and that they probably now knew she had tipped him off.

“They can’t prove it, though,” said Susan supportively.

“They have the phone records, so I expect they can,” answered Anna tearfully.

“They can’t prove what was said,” Susan offered.

“No, that’s true,” and Anna looked thoughtful. “Even if they could, would they blame me for warning Daniel?”

“Probably not. I’m sure there would be an element of sympathy, given the circumstances,” said Susan. “So what will I tell him if he phones here again?”

“Tell him I need to think things over,” said Anna. “I need time to work out if this would be a wise move for me and the girls. I can’t just go haring off to Italy on a whim, especially when the last time I saw him our marriage was over.”

“I understand,” said Susan sympathetically, “and so will Daniel.”

Back at home Anna thought about Daniel. They had said their vows and she had thought it was forever. She thought of them reuniting in Italy and starting a new life. It was not beyond the realms of possibility. She still had love for him and maybe being in a new country they could put the past behind them and start afresh. Having gone through it all in her head, she was leaning more and more towards going for it. The girls would have their father back and they would be a proper family once again.

Chapter 23

Daniel

Daniel travelled to Mondello Beach and found it every bit as beautiful as he had imagined it would be. He could see Jack loving life here. It didn't take him long to track the older man down, having stopped at a few local bars and eateries, describing Jack to staff in each one. He found Jack was well known in the community. He could imagine Jack buying the best foods and wines now.

His address was a villa on the beach and as he drove his hire car down the winding streets he saw that he lived in a gated area and had to announce himself before he could be let in. "Steve Arnold," he declared to the speaker system.

"Who?" Daniel recognised Jack's voice.

"Your old friend Steve," answered Daniel, laughing. Jack instantly recognised his laugh and pressed the buzzer. As Daniel parked up in front of the house, Jack marched out to greet him.

Over dinner and drinks, Daniel filled Jack in on all the recent events and what had led him to Sicily. Jack was looking well, deeply tanned, well dressed. His house was like a show home, filled with beautiful Italian design pieces, and he really was living the dream.

"So, Steve Arnold, eh?" said Jack after dinner. "I like it. What's your plan now, Steve?"

"Well, I'm hoping to settle here for a while, get my own place. I'm hoping Anna and the girls will join me and we can start a new life," he answered thoughtfully.

"That's a turnaround," said Jack, looking surprised. "Well, good for you, it would be great for you to get your family back. In the meantime, why don't you stay with me? I've plenty of room, as you can see. I can show you around. We can go into Palermo for a day trip. It's fantastic, you'll love it," he enthused. He appeared genuinely pleased to see Daniel. Despite their unfortunate first meeting, it seemed he now considered Daniel a friend, after all they had been through together.

Chapter 24

Sarah Harding

Sarah rang Anna's bell and stood waiting in the rain for her to answer. When Anna opened the door and saw her standing there her face fell. "Oh hi," she said, not smiling. "Come in out the rain." Gratefully, Sarah entered the warm house and took off her wet coat, handing it to Anna before following her into the kitchen, where they sat down together at the table.

"I'll cut to the chase," began Sarah. "Your phone records show you made several calls to a number in Canada. On calling the number I spoke to a girl named Grace; she confirmed she was living there with Daniel." Anna's face paled at this news and she looked genuinely shocked.

"Grace? Who the hell is Grace?" she asked angrily.

"Well, she said she was his girlfriend and that they had been living together for several months, both studying at the same art college. The point is Anna, you knew where Daniel was the whole time and, more than that, you called him the day I came round to tell you about the witness to Reggie's murder." Anna's face paled even further and she looked on the verge of tears.

"It is true, I did," she confessed to the officer. "I'm so sorry, I warned him because he killed Reggie for me, for what he did to me, and I felt I owed it to him."

"I can understand that to a certain extent," the officer said generously. “However, you’ve broken the law Anna, you could go to jail.”

“Please no! The girls! There would be no-one to look after them,” as Anna pleaded with Sarah, her tears started to fall.

“I can make this go away if you just tell me where he is now,” said Sarah, looking her straight in the eye.

“I honestly don’t know,” replied Anna, managing to maintain eye contact. She was so angry at Daniel. He’d had a girlfriend she knew nothing about – but she was not prepared to give him up to the police. “After I warned him about the witness Daniel said he must leave Canada and it would not be safe for him to contact me again. Our marriage is over. I don’t want to see him again,” she said convincingly. Looking into her eyes, Sarah believed her.

“In that case, I think there is nothing left to do here,” Sarah said despondently. “My investigation has gone cold. Daniel could be anywhere and my department doesn’t have the kind of money that would allow me to search the world for him.”

“And my tipping him off?” asked Anna, hardly able to breathe.

“I didn’t hear that. Now, show me to the door and have a happy life, Anna.” Anna heaved a great sigh of relief and happily showed the officer out.

Once the door was closed, she sagged behind it. Daniel

had a girlfriend in Canada. She was shocked at how much this revelation hurt her. There was no way she was going to Italy now. Her marriage was over. She had got away with warning Daniel and that was the last thing she would do for him. It was now time for her to concentrate on herself and her girls. She never wanted to see Daniel again.

Chapter 25

Daniel

Daniel loved living with Jack again, and he could see how happy he was with his life. Daniel was glad he had played a part in helping him live his dream. They ate well, swam in Jack's garden pool and took Jack's boat out, stopping to dive into the sea, followed by a seafood lunch and Champagne. For the short time Jack had been there he had made many friends and acquaintances. He was well liked and admired. Daniel could imagine a big house for himself, Anna and the girls, and the thought cheered him.

Daniel called Susan to find out if Anna had made up her mind to join him. "Hey Susan," he said casually. "Have you heard from Anna?"

"Daniel," said Susan, sounding on edge; he sensed she did not have good news for him. "About Anna – she had a visit from the police last week, and they told her they had called your number in Canada and Grace informed them you'd left already." She waited for his response but was unsurprised that there was silence.

Daniel realised that Anna finding out about a girlfriend he had elected not to tell her about had probably not gone down very well. "Ah, I see," he said eventually. "So I take it she does not want to join me then?"

"Correct," said Susan, unemotionally. "She nearly got arrested for tipping you off Daniel, and it came as a huge shock to her that you were in another relationship."

"I know, I understand," he said sadly. "Can you just tell Anna I will always love her and the girls and maybe one day I will see them again?"

"I'll do that, Daniel," she answered coldly. "Oh, and one more thing. Anna said to tell you the case has gone cold so you can relax." And Susan put down the receiver.

Daniel was gutted. His dreams of Anna and the girls joining him in Italy had just been smashed to pieces. Daniel had to accept that they would never be together again. It was a hard blow. He consoled himself with the fact that if they had joined him they might have led the police to him and an unhappy ending would have been the fate of them all. He joined Jack and told him the news.

Jack seemed almost as gutted as Daniel; but he was also pragmatic. "Never mind, Daniel," he consoled him. "It would probably have been too dicey for Anna to bring the kids here. Look on it as a new life for you. I know it's not what you envisaged but you began a new life in Canada and you can do it again here. Did I tell you there are some wealthy visitors here? They like playing cards; are you any good at cards?"

Daniel looked quickly at Jack, and saw that familiar

twinkle in his eye. Daniel had a feeling they were about to embark on a new challenge and the thought excited him.

Part 3

Chapter 1

Daniel

It was early morning and the beach was deserted as Daniel ambled along, cutting a solitary figure as he kicked at the pebbles and broken stones. He stooped to pick up a flat stone and skimmed it along the water's surface. The stone bounced several times, before gravity took hold and sunk it into the seabed. He watched the gentle ebb and flow of the tide as his thoughts turned to home – as they often did.

He wondered what Anna and the girls were doing. He kept in contact through Susan; he still never dared to telephone the house in case the police were still keeping tabs. He was happy to hear they were all doing well and the girls seemed to be thriving at school and activities. Leah was a keen swimmer. Daniel had learned that she was taking part in many competitions around the country. Eloise, an animal lover, was excelling in all her classes and had aspirations of becoming a vet when she left school. She was certainly clever enough.

Daniel despaired at how much he'd missed of his daughters growing up, and felt like he had really let them down. Daniel and Anna had decided to tell the girls that he was living in Italy now and that they had separated; they didn't ask many questions and seemed to accept it.

He missed being home. Looking at the broken stones on

the beach he began picking them up and throwing them into the sea. He wondered if they would travel and be washed up somewhere else. He wondered for a minute whether, if he threw himself in the sea, he would end up somewhere else; home perhaps. But he could never return.

∞

Daniel had been living in Mondello Beach with Jack for just over two years now. He could barely believe it had been that long; time had flown by. It had been a fairly enjoyable two years. The pair got on well, they lived like kings and had no money worries dragging them down, thanks to their art forgeries and, more recently, their card scamming business, which was more for their entertainment than anything else.

The scam was the Three Card Monte, also known as 'Find the Lady' or the 'Three Card Trick'. Basically it started off with three cards; they used the Jack, King and Queen of Hearts. Jack would expertly shuffle all three cards, keeping a firm track of where the Queen was at all times before laying the three cards face down on the table. A wager would be set and the mark, the victim, would have to point out the Queen. Jack would then fix his gaze on one of the other cards, misleading the victim into thinking that was the Queen. Nine out of ten times they would fall for it.

It was easy money. Sometimes they would let the victim

win so that the scam was not so obvious, but always at the end of the game, when lots of alcohol had been consumed, they would up the ante and the wager, walking away at the end with a handshake, which left the baffled player wondering where it had all gone wrong. It had kept them entertained and they had met a host of interesting characters along the way.

However, during quiet moments Daniel felt low. He would reflect on how his life had turned out. Memories of his father's cruelty were never far from his mind, memories he could not erase no matter how hard he tried. He had always hoped to be a wonderful father, kind, caring, understanding, but now, because of his circumstances, he could not be a father at all and this really depressed him. He had always wanted an honest, hardworking life, with a happy family, and he had that for a while before Reggie had resurfaced and ruined everything.

Thinking back to his days in Afghanistan was painful. He still felt shame when he thought back to that awful night during the village search, when his men were brutally killed by the Taliban; when he remained frozen upstairs. The memory of that night and its repercussions would haunt him forever.

He often wondered whether, if he had been a hero that night, things would have turned out differently. Maybe he and Reggie would even have become friends. He highly doubted this, however; there was something in Reggie that just made him a bad guy. He did not doubt that for a minute. But what was he, himself? He was a criminal, hiding from the law. He was a master forger, he had become rich by ill-gotten gains, he had murdered a man – and that fact was the most painful to swallow.

The memory of that awful day when he had been left with no choice but to push Reggie in front of a bus would always be a black cloud over him. If he hadn't done it Reggie would have always been in his life, ruining anything good he had, and Daniel knew this. He still felt sick to the stomach that he had taken the man's life. Not overtly religious, he did, however, believe in God and he had prayed for forgiveness every single night since the horrible incident occurred.

Daniel worried constantly that he had committed such a heinous crime. Sometimes he felt being separated from his family, his home and his country was the price he had to pay for his sin. It bothered him that he and Jack were still living dishonestly by scamming people at cards. Somehow he felt too far gone for redemption. An honest, happy life was beyond his grasp now; maybe in the next life he could be the person he wanted to be.

In the time they had spent together, Jack had opened up a lot more about his life. His wife had died of cancer after a short battle with the disease. Daniel had been surprised to hear this; Jack had never mentioned his wife until now. They had been teenage sweethearts, had a happy marriage. Sylvia had been happy to follow Jack around during his career in the army. They had a son, Gareth, who kept Sylvia busy and happy. They both doted on their boy, he was the centre of their world. They had given him everything, and willingly.

When Gareth was twenty he met the love of his life, Rebecca – and that was when they began to lose their boy. Rebecca was only interested in her family and friends. She showed no interest in Jack and Sylvia at all. Sylvia was heartbroken when, year after year, the pair would spend their holidays and Christmases with Rebecca's family. As time went on, she would hear from her son only through the occasional phone call.

Jack had been too busy with his career to be too much affected by their son's absence. It cut him to the quick when he did dwell on it and he hated seeing Sylvia so upset. It broke his heart and angered him. He thought his son was weak for not standing up to Rebecca, for not insisting on seeing his parents. The anger was easier than the hurt so Jack continued to be furious with Gareth.

When Sylvia was diagnosed with terminal cancer and had only weeks to live, Jack reached out to Gareth, thinking surely he would come running to be at his mother's side in her final weeks. Shockingly, and unforgivably, Gareth did not come to see his mother and Jack cut him off at that moment. He no longer had a son.

When Gareth did not even attend his mother's funeral, it confirmed that the boy was dead to him. He felt like he had not only lost his wife and best friend. He had also buried his son that day. This was the first time in years that he had told anyone he had a son.

Daniel felt closer to Jack now he had opened up and began to understand him more. It was funny how it had turned out; there was Daniel with no relationship with his father, having stopped talking to him years ago because of the abuse he had suffered at his hands as a youth, and here was Jack having no relationship with his son. Daniel was forty-two and Jack would be sixty-eight this summer. They were often mistaken for father and son. Jack had given Daniel the biggest compliment ever when he told him he would've been more than proud if Daniel had been his son. They each filled a gap in the other's life and had a mutual respect for one another.

Chapter 2

Anna

Anna was happy enough. The girls were thriving and didn't seem too adversely affected by their father's absence. Leah's swimming practice kept them all busy. Anna had to get up very early to take Leah to the pool for practice. Then back home for breakfast before dropping them both off at school. She then headed to the salon to work all day cutting and styling clients' hair. She lived her life around the girls' schedules. She always put them first. Being a single parent she wanted them to feel secure, important and loved – and they did.

Anna rarely thought about Daniel and it no longer upset her that he was out of their lives. She had totally blocked out the whole Reggie incident. Reggie did not exist and never had in Anna's mind.

Rachel and Susan, her best friends, were both trying to convince her that it was time she met someone new. She couldn't imagine herself meeting anyone just now. All her time was used up on the girls and any alone time she got, she treasured. Maybe she would meet someone one day in the future, but not yet.

She knew Daniel was kept up to date about her and the girls' lives by Susan. She was happy to hear news about him, just to know that he was alright. That was as far as communications went between them. She knew if she ever did meet anyone else he would have to love her girls as much as she did and put them first. That was a tall order and in reality she did not think such a man existed. She put the idea of meeting one firmly out her mind.

Her parents played a big part in her life. They had been sorely disappointed and shocked when Daniel and she split up.

Anna had kept them in the dark about the real reasons the marriage fell apart, so they could only assume he'd had an affair or something dramatic like that. They respected Anna's silence on the subject and were happy to be on hand when she needed a babysitter or support in any way. They were pleasantly surprised to be told that Daniel had made sure they had plenty of money from the sale of his artwork, and that he continued to support them financially from wherever he was. As long as Anna and the girls were okay – that was their main concern.

Anna loved her work in the salon. She was a talented hairdresser and had a list of loyal customers who came back to her time and time again. She gained new clients also. The salon was busy from the time she started until she left in the evenings. She loved every minute of it. She got a lot of satisfaction from her work and although she did not need the money, having been left very well off by Daniel's contribution and continued financial support, she had no intention of giving up her work. The money from Daniel would be used to fund the girls' future. Eloise would likely end up at university, she was so clever, and her dreams of becoming a vet would no doubt become a reality. Leah was a top young swimmer; it would come as no surprise if she ended up winning gold at the Olympics some day. She was so proud of them both, they were a joy to be around.

∞

It was a normal busy Saturday morning at the salon, when a young man entered the shop. He spoke to Julie on reception and asked if he could be fitted in for a cut. Anna had just finished applying the foils to her client's hair, so would have half an hour before they needed taking out. She agreed to cut the customer's hair.

He was very attractive. Tall, with thick, dark brown hair in need of tidying up. Green eyes with a hint of mischief in them, and lush full lips. He was well dressed, in a turtleneck, smart trousers and brogues. Anna loved a man in brogues and approved of how well this young man had put himself together. They chatted with ease while Anna cut and styled his hair. He told her his name was Michael and that he worked as a teaching assistant in a primary school. He loved kids and volunteered at a local youth centre at the weekends. She was impressed and suddenly felt bashful.

He also told her he loved sports, mainly swimming, and that he adored animals. He had always wanted a dog but his parents would never allow it, and now he was too busy to have one.

"So how about you? I've told you almost everything there is to know about me," Michael looked at her in the mirror, laughing.

"Well, I'm Anna. I work here, obviously," she answered giggling, "I have two gorgeous girls, one who funnily enough excels in swimming and the other a complete animal lover. You'd get on well with them both." She blushed furiously at this presumptuous statement. What was she thinking?

The truth was, she was mesmerised by this attractive stranger and was loving the conversation. He seemed to be a good ten years younger than her. But they gelled and, for the first time since Daniel left, she felt like maybe she could like someone that way again.

"They sound like great kids," answered Michael thoughtfully. "Their father, is he on the scene?"

"No, they no longer see their dad," she answered. "I no longer see him, to be honest, and it's taken a while but we're all fine with it."

"Oh, that's good," replied Michael. "I see so many kids at the school from broken homes and it can really affect them badly. You must be doing a great job as a single parent. Good for you," and he smiled generously.

Once she had finished drying his newly cut and styled hair,

she led him to reception to take payment. As he handed over his credit card, he looked at her shyly.

"I don't suppose you would let me take you out for dinner one day?" he asked with a smile.

Anna blushed furiously and smiled up at him. "Yeah, why not, that would be really nice." She stood watching him walk down the street, arms folded across her body and with a huge beam on her face.

"Wow," said Julie. "He's something else. Look at you, you're like the cat that got the cream."

On the way home, Anna popped in to the store for wine and nibbles. Rachel and Susan were coming round for a few drinks and a catch up. She couldn't wait to tell them about Michael. They would be shocked and pleased.

She thought about the girls, and decided not to mention him to them until she got to know him a bit better. Maybe this dinner would be the one and only date they had – there was no point telling them just now anyway. She almost skipped home. She felt young and happy. At thirty-six, she wasn't exactly old. She figured Michael to be in his mid-twenties. Was it too big an age gap? she fretted. But she was getting ahead of herself again. She would just play it by ear, see how things went, take it slowly.

Before her friends arrived, Anna took a good look at herself in the bedroom mirror – something she hadn't really done in a while. More interested in the girls and everything to do with them, she had let herself go a bit. She still made sure she was always smartly dressed for work but as for taking her time with her makeup and buying anything new… well, that had slipped.

She took her time and applied her makeup expertly, drawing on the dark cat's eye corner with expert precision, applying a smear of grey eye shadow, followed by thick dark mascara. She stepped back and scrutinised herself in the mirror. She looked good. Her dark hair shone, thanks to the endless supply of top-of-the-range shampoo and conditioners from the salon. The smoky look really suited her small heart-shaped face. She was in good shape physically, thanks to all the running around she did after the girls and being on her feet all day at work.

All round she was quite happy with herself. She felt she looked younger than her thirty-six years; that she and Michael could easily pass for a couple without eyebrows being raised about the age difference. She laughed out loud at herself getting way ahead again, then finished getting dressed just as the doorbell rang.

Anna ran down the stairs and answered the door to Rachel and Susan, who had uncharacteristically arrived at the same time.

"Hi," she enthused, grabbing them in big hugs and kisses. "Come in out of the cold."

"You look fabulous," said Susan, taking off her coat and

handing it to Anna.

"Yes, you really do," agreed Rachel, taking in the happy glow of her dear friend, something she had not seen for a while.

"What's happened?" asked Susan, suddenly suspicious. "Something's happened. You look glowing. Have you had good news?"

Anna was laughing, hanging up their coats and ushering them into the kitchen, where the table was set with wine glasses and a cheese board with olives. The lights were set low and candles illuminated the room, creating a lovely peaceful atmosphere. In the background, chill-out songs played from a speaker in the corner. Anna had the room decked out prettily with shades of lemon and grey.

She poured her friends generous glasses of chilled wine, then they all seated themselves around the table.

"So," enquired Rachel. "Spill the beans then."

"What beans?" exclaimed Anna, shocked at her friends' gossip radar. Nothing escaped this pair. "You two, what are you like? There are no beans to spill," she protested, but laughing.

"Then what's with the happy glow?" Susan pressed, helping herself to some crackers and cheese.

"I'm just in a happy place right now," said Anna, taking a sip of wine. "The girls are doing great, I've no financial worries at the moment, work's great, life is good."

"Ah, so no news then," said Rachel, looking disappointed. "I could have sworn you had something to share with the group," she added mischievously.

"No, no news," replied Anna, watching their faces closely as she added, "except that I got myself a date." Then she doubled up with laughter.

"I knew it!" exclaimed Susan, almost choking on her cracker.

"Tell all," bossed Rachel, with her hands on hips. Then she pushed her elbows further on the table to listen better.

"Well, a very handsome young man came into the salon on Saturday. His name is Michael, he's a teaching assistant, he loves kids, swimming and animals." Her eyes were shining with happiness.

"He is perfect for you!" said Susan, with a sudden serious expression on her face. "Thank you, God," she added, hands together in prayer, eyes to the ceiling.

"And he sounds like he'd be a huge hit with the girls, with those interests," added Rachel happily. "When's the big date?"

"Saturday night," Anna told them, holding her hands up to her face. "What am I going to wear? He's a bit younger than me, I think mid-twenties. Is that too young? Am I a cougar?" She was full of doubt now she had actually voiced her fears.

"No, don't be silly, you look like you're that age," Susan

consoled her. “Let’s go shopping Saturday morning and get you looking even more fabulous.”

The rest of the evening was spent in a jovial manner, discussing Michael and the upcoming date. It was light-hearted and fun. Anna went to bed laughing at the girls’ enthusiasm, feeling happy and excited at the thought of Saturday night.

On Saturday morning, Anna dropped Leah at swimming practice, then Eloise at her friend’s house, before heading into town to meet the girls. Susan had offered to have the girls for tea and a sleepover, so that Anna could enjoy her date without worrying about them. She told them she was going to a work’s night out, not wanting to admit it was a date at this early stage.

She greeted Susan and Rachel enthusiastically, and the trio headed to the fashion shops in search of a knock-out outfit for Anna. After trying on hundreds of outfits, she opted for a pair of black satin, loose-fitting trousers. They hung off her slight waist seductively, and they chose an off-the-shoulder silver top with sparkly silver sandals to match. To complete the outfit, she bought silver drop earrings and a simple silver bracelet, with silver clutch. She felt great in the outfit and could not thank the girls enough for their input.

After a delicious lunch, the girls surprised her with a voucher to a local beauty salon – she had been booked in for several beauty treatments. She was touched and delighted. Susan said she would pick up the girls and that she had a fun-packed afternoon planned for them. Anna could pick them up at her house the next day.

∞

Anna felt a million dollars as she entered the small Thai restaurant that evening. The atmosphere was cosy and dimly lit. She saw Michael immediately. He looked devastatingly handsome in a black turtleneck, checked trousers and smart black shoes. He made his way to greet her and led her to the table

"You look stunning," he appraised her, kissing her on each cheek.

"Thank you," she smiled. "You don't look so bad yourself." Michael had already ordered a bottle of rosé wine, and he poured her a glass while they waited for their food.

She felt as nervous as a teenager on her very first date, as he gazed at her with his green eyes.

"I've not stopped thinking of you since we met on Saturday," he admitted shyly.

"I've thought about you a lot, too," replied Anna, taking a sip of wine. "This is the first date I've been on since Daniel left. I'm not sure I'm ready for anything heavy," she told him honestly. "The girls have to be my priority. As their only parent I always put them first." She felt it was important to tell him now. If it bothered him he could get out now and no-one would get hurt. She looked at him to see how this news affected him, but he was smiling and took hold of her hands on the table.

"That's wonderful," he said, "it just makes me like you even more. Let's take things slowly, be friends first. I'd love to meet the girls, talk to Leah about her swimming, take them to the zoo." He was laughing now.

"The zoo?" questioned Anna. "Is that more for you than the girls?" she added, laughing.

"You can read me like a book," he grinned. "I also thought we could all go horse riding, since I love animals and Eloise loves animals."

"You've really thought this all through," said Anna, thinking what a sweet guy he was. He seemed to have no problem with taking things slowly, and she was so grateful he was taking such an interest in the girls.

The rest of the evening was delightful. The food was beautiful and delicate, the conversation flowed easily. At the end of the night, Michael hailed a taxi for her and did not suggest going home with her, which she appreciated. He gave her a goodnight kiss on the cheek and said he would call her soon. She was on cloud nine when she got home. As she snuggled up in her bed, she thought this could be the start of something really special.

Chapter 3

Daniel & Jack

Daniel and Jack had spent another gorgeous day on the ocean in Jack's boat, *Lucky Lady*. They had swum, fished and enjoyed a tasty lunch. They were tired when they got back to Jack's beach house, and each pulled up a sun lounger by the pool to doze the rest of the day away. Jack fell asleep almost immediately. Daniel scanned him lazily; he was a bit worried about Jack.

Recently he seemed to be increasingly forgetful, always losing his keys, not remembering names. He couldn't follow plots very well if they ever watched a drama series together. Just the other night they had been watching one of their favourites on catch up, the main character a World War One veteran who had been scarred by the horrors of war. Back home, the main character and his family became a criminal gang, hunted down by a keen Irish policeman, who had made it his mission in life to put an end to the family's criminal affairs.

"I don't understand what Arthur's got to do with it," Jack said, looking perplexed.

"Arthur's Tommy's brother," Daniel told him. Bloody hell, Arthur was one of the main characters and one of their favourites; Daniel didn't get Jack's confusion.

"Oh yes, of course he is," laughed Jack, brushing it off.

Daniel could tell Jack was not following the story at all and spent the rest of the programme watching Jack.

It wasn't like him. Normally he was sharp as a tack. Perhaps it was nothing to worry about, he could just be tired, but Daniel decided to keep an eye on him and take note of any more worrying behaviours.

∞

They went to their favourite tavern for a meal. It was busy, as usual, and the atmosphere was friendly and laid-back. There were a lot of new faces; visitors to the beach. Jack decided they should get the cards out. They played together for a while, Daniel acting the part of winning each time, and played with a bit of money, too, so that they would draw some attention. They didn't have to wait long before a stranger asked for a game. After an hour or so, and having faced a hefty loss, the stranger departed sheepishly.

Daniel scanned the room to see if anyone else had shown interest in playing. His eyes fell upon a good-looking couple. The man was tall, had chiselled cheek bones and a hard stare. He looked to be in his mid-forties. The young lady beside him was breathtakingly stunning. She had raven black hair down to her waist, big brown eyes and a perfect figure. She looked stylish and well off, as did the man she was with. The man seemed to be interested in the card game, and as Daniel caught his eye, the man stood up and made his way over to them.

"Hi," he said, extending his hand towards Jack for a shake, then Daniel. "I'm Tommy and this is my daughter, Eve." Eve nodded their way, before quietly taking a seat beside her father.

"Hi," replied Jack. "Are you on holiday here?"

"Yes, we've just come down to get a break from the city for a couple of weeks," Tommy told them. "Can I buy you gentlemen a drink?"

"Let me," said Daniel, rising from the table. "And the lady?"

"Just water for me, thank you," Eve replied coyly, fluttering her lovely long lashes at Daniel. His heart skipped a beat.

"I'm Jack," said Jack, introducing himself to the pair. "That's Steve," Daniel heard him add as he made his way to the bar.

Daniel still went by the name Steve, the name he chose when he fled Canada. You never knew who you were talking to and they still needed to be wary.

"So, what line of business are you in, Tommy?" enquired Jack.

"Oh, this and that. Mainly financial affairs," Tommy answered evasively, clearly not wanting to go into details. Jack didn't mind. He was only making conversation; he didn't want the man's life story.

Daniel returned to the tables with the drinks. The four chatted amicably about Mondello Beach, fishing, restaurant recommendations. It was easy conversation, light-hearted and amusing.

Daniel found it difficult not to stare at Eve too much; she was so beautiful, spoke eloquently and was an absolute delight to be around.

Tommy indicated that he would very much like a game of cards. Jack let him win the first few games to get his confidence up. Because they were likely to see Tommy and Eve again, Jack did not take him for much on this first night. The stakes were never very high. Tommy seemed happy enough to have lost some, won some. The night ended on a happy note, with all parties agreeing to see each other at the tavern again some night. Jack told them this was their favourite haunt and they would find them there most evenings.

Back at home, Daniel and Jack had a drink and chatted about their evening. "That girl, though," Daniel said dreamily, "I can't get her face out of my mind, what a beauty."

"Ah, she was indeed," reflected Jack, in agreement. "She was one of a kind. That brother of hers, though, I'm not so sure. He seemed a bit evasive."

"Brother? That was her father," Daniel corrected,

disbelievingly.

"Did I say brother?" laughed Jack. "I meant father."

Daniel looked at him hard; yes, he was worried about Jack.

∞

Jack was definitely getting worse; he had started calling Daniel Gareth. He'd aimlessly wander into rooms and forget what he was there for. More than once he had flooded the bathroom, leaving the tap running for a bath, then going out somewhere. Daniel decided to broach the subject of a visit to the doctor. There was no getting away from it.

Jack did not take the news well. He didn't think there was anything wrong with him, and made it plain he thought visiting the doctor was a total waste of time. But Daniel insisted and made an appointment for the following day.

"So, what's been happening with you then?" asked Dr Rossi, looking at Jack with concern.

"Absolutely nothing, doctor. Steve here insisted I came to see you, but for the life of me I can't think why," answered Jack, giving Daniel a sideways glance. Daniel was relieved he remembered to call him Steve. Dr Rossi looked at Daniel for answers.

"Well, Jack has been very forgetful lately. He loses his keys on a daily basis, has flooded the bathroom on more than one occasion, forgets he's running a bath then goes out somewhere.

He calls me Gareth, his son's name. He doesn't seem to be able to follow plot lines very well, when we are watching TV programmes or films," Daniel looked sad, as he gave the doctor as much information as he could think of.

"We all forget things from time to time," said Dr Rossi sympathetically. "But this does seem a bit more than the occasional memory loss." He began tapping away on his keyboard, squinting at his computer screen. "I'd like to make an appointment for you with a specialist, just to get an accurate assessment of you, Jack. It's nothing to worry about," he added, when he saw the look of concern cross Jack's face. Daniel looked relieved; he was very worried about his friend and only wanted to help him.

They were given an appointment to see a psychiatrist the following week, to assess Jack further and hopefully give him a diagnosis. In the meantime, Daniel was to keep a diary of any unusual behaviour so he could give the doctor a better idea of what was going on.

"There's nothing wrong with me," huffed Jack on the drive home.

"Well there's nothing for you to worry about then, is there?" Daniel retorted. Changing the subject, he suggested lunch at Jack's favourite eatery overlooking the harbour. As they waited for their food, Daniel appraised his friend. He was still a handsome looking man for his age. Sixty-eight this summer, since moving to Italy Jack was looking remarkably well. Tanned and trim on their Mediterranean diet, with plenty of exercise, walking and swimming, it was devastating to think there could be something seriously wrong with him. Daniel put it out of his mind and gazed out the window at the golden beach and sea. They were lucky to have found such a great spot to live.

Chapter 4

Anna

Things were going great with Michael. They had been on several more dates before Anna decided it was time she introduced him to her daughters. He had been so keen to meet them, she felt she could no longer put it off.

"So I have this friend, Michael," she told Leah and Eloise, whilst they ate their tea at the table. "He's very keen to visit the zoo, being an animal lover, but he doesn't want to go alone. Would you girls fancy going?"

"What, just us?" asked Leah, incredulously.

"No, silly, I'd go too, of course," laughed Anna.

"Yes!" shouted Eloise excitedly, "I love the zoo, when are we going?"

"How about this Saturday after swimming practice?" Anna suggested. She realised she was holding her breath, waiting to see if Leah would want to join them.

"Um, yeah okay," Leah answered unenthusiastically. "Whatever."

"I'm so excited," enthused Eloise, a total contrast to her sister. "I actually cannot wait."

Anna began clearing the tea things away, humming happily to herself. It was happening. The girls were going to meet Michael. She prayed they would love him as much as she did. She thought Eloise would be easily won over but Leah was going through that awkward teenage stage and was a tougher nut to crack.

Michael was over the moon when she called him later to tell him the girls were keen to meet him and go to the zoo. She left out Leah's lack of enthusiasm. He'd soon see she was just a normal teenager who needed a fair amount of cajoling before she came round. She wasn't overly worried about it. After all, Michael worked at school so would be used to children and their ways.

When Saturday arrived, Eloise wanted to go to the zoo as soon as she got up. "Leah has swimming practice first," laughed Anna, making them breakfast.

"Oh, do you have to go to stupid practice?" whined Eloise, her face scrunching up in despair.

"Duh, obviously," retorted Leah. "I think my swimming is a tad more important than the stupid zoo," she added, slamming her towel into her sports bag, while munching on toast.

"Of course it is," soothed Anna, keen to smooth things over. She did not want the girls at loggerheads on their first meeting with Michael. It'd be enough to scare him off. "Come on, hurry up or we'll be late," she fussed the girls out the door and safely into the car.

While they waited for Leah, Anna and Eloise had hot

chocolate and a muffin in the swimming centre's cafe. The time dragged by and eventually Leah came out of the changing room, her long brown hair still dripping from the pool.

"You should have dried your hair, Leah," Anna chided, thinking it wasn't exactly a warm day for walking about the zoo with wet hair.

"It's fine," her daughter answered, tutting under her breath.

"It's not fine, you'll get rheumatics in your head," Anna replied, not fully knowing what that meant. Her mother always said it to her when she was a teenager.

"Whatever, who cares, I don't even know what that means," replied Leah, trudging out of the centre.

The teenager was tall for her age and thin as a rake. Dressed inleggings and an oversized sweatshirt, she looked easily like she could be a model. Swimming was her main priority in life.

Eloise was shorter than her sister, with golden curls down to her shoulder. She had wide blue eyes that seemed to shine with amazement at new things and she was still at that easy-going, easy-to-please stage. For that, Anna was thankful. One sultry teenager at a time, she could handle.

Michael was waiting for them at the zoo's entrance and excitedly waved as the three approached. "Hi girls," he enthused,

"I've been so looking forward to meeting you and so excited about seeing all the animals."

"Me too," chipped in Eloise, accepting the warm hug from Michael. Leah shrugged him off awkwardly, but managed a smile and a shy hello. After purchasing their tickets, the girls went on ahead, Eloise excitedly going from one enclosure to another, whilst Leah grudgingly followed.

"Well, what do you think of my girls?" Anna asked Michael when they were out of earshot.

"They are great," he answered. "Just like their mother of course and Eloise is so enthusiastic, isn't she?"

"Yes, she was so excited to come. Leah is a teenager, of course," she excused. "She won't show how much she's enjoying herself because that wouldn't be cool," and she laughed.

"Of course not," Michael said solemnly. "How uncool to actually enjoy a visit to the zoo."

He grabbed her hand and pulled her close for a kiss. Her eyes searched for the girls and noticing they had their backs to them, gave him a quick peck on the lips. "They think we are just friends," she told him. "One step at a time."

"Yes, of course, I agree," answered Michael, leaving her side and running to catch up with the girls. He joined Eloise excitedly pointing out the animals, and the pair took selfies and at least a hundred photos. Leah fell into step with her mother and complained about her legs being sore with all the walking up and down the hills. All in all, it was a successful day and they finished off by going for a pizza for tea, Leah's favourite.

Back at home, Anna quizzed the girls on their thoughts of Michael. "He's so nice!" Eloise was already a big fan, mainly because, like her, Michael loved animals.

"He's alright," Leah added unconvincingly. "What's the big deal? It's not like he's your boyfriend or anything." Anna went bright red, which did not go unnoticed by Leah and this annoyed her. "Or is he?" she demanded.

"No, he's not," Anna denied it immediately, "Michael and I are just friends."

"I should hope so; you're still married to Dad aren't you?" Leah asked innocently.

"I am still married to your father, on paper only. When we can, we will probably get divorced; I've told you this already." Anna was taken aback by Leah mentioning Daniel. The girls rarely said his name at all.

"He's too young for you anyway," Leah said nastily and slammed the door on her way to bed. Anna felt as though she'd been slapped in the face, and she stood stock still, staring at the slammed door.

What had been a lovely day had now turned sour. They had never really discussed Daniel, the girls showing no interest in where their dad was or what he was doing. Anna assumed it was because they remembered how bad things were when Daniel was on his downward spiral, getting drunk all the time, not being there for them; and then how much happier they all were when he left. Now she wondered if they remembered the bad bits at all.

Daniel had wanted to keep in contact with them but it was too difficult and dangerous, should the police be keeping tabs on them; and no-one knew. The only contact he had with the girls was through Susan and Anna, and they had only ever spoken to Daniel once since he had moved to Italy. Anna did not feel the need to speak to him, still angry at finding out he had a girlfriend in Canada. She was happy for him to get on with his life and leave her to get on with hers.

But Leah bringing her father up made Anna worry that she would soon want to see him, talk to him, want him back in her life. She would have to cross that bridge when they came to it. She sighed. Why was life always so complicated?

Chapter 5

Daniel & Jack

As they ate their delicious seafood lunch and drank crisp, white wine, Daniel noticed Tommy and Eve enter the tavern. A smile lit up his face, as he waved them over. “Hi, come and sit with us,” he suggested, pulling up two chairs to their table. Eve looked beautiful, fresh and young in a white t-shirt and denim shorts, teamed with white training shoes. Tommy looked casual, too, in shorts and t-shirt. They looked happy and relaxed.

“Thank you,” said Tommy as he joined them. “That food looks delicious, I think we’ll have some of that.” He looked at Eve, who nodded her agreement.

“I’m ravenous,” she agreed. “We’ve just been on a ten-mile walk,” she told Daniel and Jack. “It’s so beautiful, though, it wasn’t exactly a hardship,” she added, smiling.

“I’m glad we ran into you,” said Tommy, “I need to return to the city for a few days, a business matter. Would it be an imposition if I asked you to keep Eve entertained and safe for me?”

“Of course,” Daniel answered immediately. He was delighted at the thought of keeping Eve entertained. She was clearly far too young for him, but he couldn’t help the feelings she instilled in him. He was like a teenager with a crush.

“Our hotel isn’t too far from your place. Maybe if you

could just meet her there when you are going somewhere and make sure you take her back." Tommy looked concerned, as if he was second guessing leaving his daughter in the hands of these men he barely knew.

"Don't worry," Jack said quickly, as if reading his mind. "She is in safe hands. We will absolutely look after her."

Tommy visibly relaxed. The food arrived and they enjoyed their lunch. The conversation flowed well after that, as they discussed things to do in Tommy's absence.

∞

The next day, Daniel intended to pick Eve up at the hotel and take her out on the *Lucky Lady*. Jack said he was tired and would spend the day attending to some paperwork and relaxing. He wanted to check his citizenship details over. After being in Italy for a year, Jack had applied for citizenship. It had cost him a pretty penny. He had no intention of returning to the UK and he wanted to make sure he would not have any problems with the Italian authorities. Daniel was worried about him. Jack insisted he was fine and sent him on his way.

Eve looked beautiful, as usual. She was wearing a strappy floral summer dress she had made herself, with her swimsuit underneath. She had packed a towel, fully expecting to go swimming at some point during their day. "You look stunning," said Daniel, smiling as she got in the car beside him.

"Thank you," she replied coyly. "I'm so looking forward to today, I absolutely adore the sea."

"Me too," said Daniel. "I thought we could do some fishing, have a swim followed by a lovely seafood lunch."

"Fantastic," enthused Eve, gazing out of the window happily. The smell of her coconut sunscreen filled the air.

It was a beautiful day. The water was calm. They fished for a while, catching nothing but small fish they happily released back into the sea.

They jumped off the boat at the highest point and swam to a small cove, where they sat for a while. "So, tell me a bit about yourself," said Daniel, as they lay enjoying the sun's rays drying off their wet skin.

"Not much to tell really," laughed Eve, "I was brought up in Northampton. My parents split up when I was eight. I have a brother who's two years older than me. We chose to stay with our dad. My mum suffered depression and was difficult to be around."

"I'm sorry to hear that," Daniel said supportively. "That must have been tough."

"Yes it was. I think she struggled when we were very young, although I don't remember that much, just what Dad tells us really. I never see my mum now; she lives with her sister in Manchester.

"Dad's always been pretty hard on me and my brother growing up. He only wants the best for us. I'm doing an undergraduate fashion degree at the moment at Northampton Uni. I love it. What about you, Steve? How come you are living on Mondello Beach with Jack?"

"Ah, it's a long story," said Daniel, sighing heavily. "Will we swim back to the boat and I'll tell you over lunch?"

"Yes, that would be fabulous," agreed Eve, heading for the water.

The lunch was delicious: fresh prawns with salad; crisp, chilled white wine; and strawberries with cream. Eating out on the deck, feeling the hot sun's rays and hearing the gentle lapping of the water lolling off the side of the boat, the pair were relaxed and happy. Daniel began to open up a little to Eve about his past.

"I have two girls back home in Yorkshire," he told her, looking sad. "I never get to see them but I'm hoping that will change in the future."

"Why do you never see them? What's happened?" asked Eve, shading her eyes from the sun's glare.

"A lot happened," admitted Daniel, apprehensively. He had to be careful what he was telling Eve, but somehow he felt at ease with her and suddenly it felt good to have someone other than Jack to talk to about his past.

"Growing up, my dad was a cruel man. He was very hard

on me. I couldn't wait to leave home and join the army. I loved the army. I was used to discipline, having been brought up by the world's harshest disciplinarian," he said, rolling his eyes. "I served in Northern Ireland and Afghanistan," and his eyes clouded over and his face fell, as if the pain of the past was creating panic in him now. "Sorry, I've never really spoken about Afghanistan to anyone, quite painful memories," he admitted.

She touched his arm softly. "It's okay, you don't have to if it's too difficult. I understand." He was able to steady himself.

"No, no it's fine really. There was an incident…" Daniel relayed the awful events that had changed him, as Eve listened intently.

"There was an inquest. I requested voluntary discharge. I had seen too much, was too shaken up by events. I just wanted out." Daniel finished his story.

"No wonder," said Eve sympathetically. "It sounds like hell on earth. What about the man in the coma, did he survive?"

"Yes, he survived, unfortunately for me," said Daniel, finishing off his wine.

"Why unfortunately for you?" Eve asked, her brown eyes wide with interest.

"Well that's a whole other story," said Daniel. "I think I better get you back now. I'll tell you another time."

Daniel dropped Eve back at her hotel for a nap and to

freshen up. He agreed to pick her up at eight for some dinner and drinks, hopefully with Jack. When he got back to the villa he found Jack asleep on the chair in the lounge. He began to stir when he heard Daniel come in.

"Hey, how did your day go?" he asked sleepily.

"It was perfect," said Daniel. "Really nice. I think I'm going to have a nap myself. I'm picking Eve up at the hotel at eight for dinner if you want to join us?"

"You know, I don't feel up to it tonight. Going through my paperwork has given me a headache," Jack told him, looking exhausted. "If you don't mind, I think I'll have an early night."

"Sure," said Daniel, surprised. It wasn't like Jack to be so tired. He was usually raring to go out in the evening. He loved socialising.

He scribbled a line in his notebook – "Jack seems to be tired all the time" – alongside the note he had made that morning – "Jack made poached eggs and put them on top of toast that had already been spread with marmalade". When Daniel had questioned him about this strange food combination, Jack merely said that was what he fancied and that was what he was having. He also called Daniel Gareth again several times, which Daniel logged in his notebook to be taken to Jack's psychiatrist appointment the following week.

Eve waited for Daniel in the hotel lobby. She wore a long,

black, flowing dress, which she again had made herself, teamed with gold jewellery. She seemed unaware of how effortlessly lovely she looked. "Steve," she said, as she rose from the couch to greet him. "You look handsome."

He was pleased, having made the extra effort to look nice for her. "You look a knock out in that dress," he replied, kissing her on both cheeks. "The restaurant is just a walk away, and it's such a nice evening."

"Great," she said, happily linking her arm in his as they made their way to the restaurant.

In the Greek restaurant, they shared some tasty starters and ordered a moussaka. "So you were telling me about yourself," said Eve, looking at him earnestly with her beautiful brown eyes.

"Oh, yes," said Daniel. "Where did I get to?"

"You got up to the bit where you said that when the man came out of his coma it was unfortunate for you."

"Oh, so you did listen," said Daniel, laughing. "Well, it was unfortunate for me because, later on in my life, this man sought me out for revenge and almost ruined me." He looked serious now, and troubled.

"How come? That sounds terrifying," asked Eve, leaning forward.

"It was. I met my wife Anna when I came out the army. We met in a nightclub when I was at college retraining and she was studying hairdressing. We got on immediately. She was – is – beautiful inside and out," Daniel's eyes lit up when he talked about Anna.

"I met her family. They were wonderful people. We were in love so the next step was marriage. It was fairly soon after we first met but it just seemed so right. Not long after, Anna fell pregnant and we had our lovely Leah, who we both adored. Anna loved being a mother, it was something she had always wanted.

"Two years later, she gave birth to Eloise. Life was good. I was working for a small firm and Anna was still hairdressing, fitting it in around the girls so she could always be there for them."

"She sounds like a wonderful lady," said Eve wistfully, thinking about the mother who had not always been there for her.

"She is," said Daniel earnestly. "The next bit is difficult to talk about," he said, wiping his brow.

"It's okay if you don't want to," said Eve sympathetically, reaching out to touch his arm in support.

He sighed deeply. "I used to buy a bacon roll for a homeless guy on the way to work every morning. One day I witnessed him being beaten up but instead of doing anything to help I turned a blind eye," he admitted regretfully. "I don't know why I didn't help. I was so regimented back then. I think it was due to my upbringing and then my military career. I just knew if I intervened, my life would somehow be in upheaval. I'd be late for work, maybe have to wait for the police, a court case that could go on for months. It sounds lame and I'm ashamed of it now. I wished I'd been a better man and just helped, you know?"

"You can't beat yourself up, Steve," said Eve kindly. "Lots of people would have done the same thing. You could have ended up getting hurt yourself."

"That's true, I suppose," he said, relieved her opinion of him had not changed with this embarrassing admission. "Anyway, I did not see the man again for a while. Then one day when I was getting off the train for work he was there, suddenly, in front of me. He shoved a note in my hand and disappeared. When I got to the office and looked at the note, it said, 'You stood by and watched me nearly die. Now I will stand by and watch you.' I was horrified, became paranoid, I didn't know what the note meant or how seriously to take it.

"I told no-one. I'm ashamed to admit it but I started drinking heavily. My work suffered, my relationship with Anna and the girls suffered. I ended up getting fired. Anna took the girls and went to stay with her friend. I lost everything in a short space of time." He became very quiet and looked down at his hands. "Then I did the unthinkable. I tried to take my own life, Eve. I got every pill we had in the house and sat at the kitchen table, downing them with vodka until I became unconscious. I was brought back to life by the homeless man. He saved me. When I asked why he did it, he said it was because I had watched him nearly die and he was going to watch me die, too." Eve could hardly breathe as Daniel related the terrible story. She was visibly shocked.

The waitress interrupted them to ask about desserts. They agreed on a cheese board and coffees, and then Eve asked what happened next.

"It turned out the homeless man was none other than Reggie Raymond Brown. The soldier who had been in a coma in Afghanistan. He was back for revenge," Daniel told her.

Eve's eyes widened in horror. "That's terrible. How frightening," she said, pulling her shawl tighter around her shoulders.

And now Daniel had revealed so much he couldn't stop the words tumbling out. "He blackmailed me, he told me he wanted me to go to an isolated farmhouse and steal two paintings worth a lot of money. Of course, I didn't want to do it but he said if I did not he would report me to the military police and a new investigation about the village raid would take place.

"I knew there was every possibility I could face prison for acts of cowardice, now that Reggie was well enough to be a witness. It was a very real threat. I could see no way out but to do as he asked. The night of the robbery, the owner woke up and held a rifle at me, tied me up and demanded to know what I was doing in his house. I told him everything. It turns out he knew Reggie, too – he was his Commanding Officer in Helmand and had been instrumental in Reggie's medical discharge. So Reggie had wanted revenge on him also. He had become a liability after coming out of the coma and was a danger to himself, the men he served with… There was no choice, Jack had to do what he had to do."

"Jack?" said Eve, her eyes widening again in surprise. "Your Jack?"

"Yes, my Jack, I suppose," laughed Daniel.

"How did you end up being such good friends?" Eve was totally enthralled by Daniel's story.

"After telling Jack my story, we tricked Reggie into coming to the farmhouse. I said I had killed the old man in a skirmish and I needed his help disposing of the body.

"When Reggie arrived, Jack held him at gun point and tied him up next to me. Jack still hadn't untied me at this point. Reggie was furious and told Jack he had ruined his life by getting him kicked out the army. Jack calmly told him if it wasn't him it would have been some other officer. Then he did a surprising thing. He offered Reggie money to disappear and stay out of both our lives. I was shocked but what other option did we have? We didn't want to kill the man. So Reggie accepted the offer but before he left he told me something that ruined my life."

Daniel looked down. The pain that suddenly overwhelmed him made him stall.

"What was it?" Eve asked softly.

"He told me he had slept with my wife," Daniel said, shrugging his shoulders, trying to shrug off the feeling his confession gave him.

"Did you believe him?" Eve asked.

"He mentioned a tattoo she has on her thigh, so yes I believed him," Daniel said, his eyes turning cold. "It ruined my marriage. When I confronted Anna, she told me he had attacked her after a night out with her girlfriends. I didn't believe her at first. Then she went to the police to report it. That's when I believed her and I hated him for it. I could not look at my wife the same way and it ruined our marriage." Daniel looked sad; Eve squeezed his hand over the table.

"How awful. What a despicable person he was," she empathised.

"Oh, he really was," said Daniel. "Yes, I made mistakes, looking back, but I never deliberately set out to hurt anyone."

It was getting late, and Daniel paid the bill. They started the walk back to Eve's hotel. "So, how did you and Jack end up such good friends? You didn't say," Eve probed.

"Well that's a whole other, other story," Daniel laughed.

"Maybe I'll tell you tomorrow, if you agree to come into the city with me. There's a gallery there you might enjoy."

"I'd love that," said Eve, smiling. "Thank you so much for a lovely dinner and such an interesting tale."

"It's my pleasure," Daniel assured her, kissing her on each cheek and waiting to see her safely into the hotel's elevator.

On the walk back to Jack's villa, Daniel felt a bit lighter. It was good to have shared his story with someone so understanding. The opinion he'd had of himself was harsh but maybe he wasn't as bad as he had thought he was. He thought about Eve. She was truly wonderful. He knew he was too old for her and that she probably only saw him as a friend. He wasn't going to go there with her. He laughed at himself – as if he'd have a chance anyway. She could have anyone of her choice. She was half his age.

Entering the villa, Daniel noticed the sliding doors to the back garden were open. He ran through, looking out into the dark night. "Jack!" he shouted, thinking at once that Jack must be out there. He ran to Jack's room and, sure enough, the bed covers were pulled back as if he'd gotten out of bed. He ran back out the sliding doors and into the expansive gardens. The gate to the street was open and he ran through them and down the street. Ahead, he saw Jack's figure shuffling along the street at a slow pace. He was out of breath by the time he'd caught up with him.

“Jack, where are you going? It’s the middle of the night!” He grasped Jack’s arm.

“Gareth,” Jack looked at him. “Where have you been, son?”

“Jack, it’s me, Daniel. I’m not Gareth,” Daniel was frustrated and worried. “Come on, let’s get you home and back to bed. Where the hell were you going at this time of night anyway?”

“I was going for a newspaper and breakfast rolls,” said Jack, looking confused.

They walked back together in silence, Jack remaining confused and Daniel exhausted with worry. There was something very wrong with Jack and it saddened him beyond comprehension.

Chapter 6

Anna

Leah continued to be difficult about Michael, much to Anna's consternation. Eloise was the total opposite – she loved Michael and adored spending time with him. Leah began spending more time at her friends' houses, rather than with her family, if Michael was going to be there. It was obvious and awkward and put Anna in a horrible position. The last thing she wanted was for Leah not to feel comfortable around them.

"Maybe you could spend some one-on-one time with her?" she suggested to Michael, desperate for the two of them to become friends.

"Maybe," said Michael, thinking about it. "I could take her for lunch in town and maybe buy her something nice?"

"She won't fall for bribery," said Anna, thinking hard. "Why don't you both go swimming, then for a lunch; try to get through to her that way?"

"Oh, I don't think so," said Michael, rejecting this plan immediately. "A lunch in town, then a treat. Ask her if she'll meet me tomorrow."

Anna was surprised that he didn't want to go swimming with Leah. After all, he had claimed to love it and that was the one thing they had in common. But she didn't push it. She felt embarrassed that he had to make this extra effort with her daughter and she was annoyed with Leah for being so difficult.

That night, she put the suggestion to Leah. She didn't jump for joy but she did, reluctantly, agree to meet him.

∞

Michael was waiting for Leah outside the cathedral, as they had planned.

"Hi," said Leah, not reaching out to him for a hug but firmly staying where she was.

"Hi," he responded, not looking overly keen to see her either. This surprised her. Normally Michael was over the top with his affection. She felt a bit unnerved. "So I thought we'd go for a walk and discuss your behaviour," Michael announced, not smiling. In fact, he was rather cold. Leah was suddenly wary and nervous. She didn't want to go for a walk with him but felt she had no other choice.

They walked in awkward silence until they came to a park. As they walked, Michael began to talk in a low, menacing voice. "Your mother and I are getting to know each other, Leah. We like each other very much and I am not going to let a spoilt little bitch ruin it." Leah looked at him in shock. He had visibly changed from the friendly pushover she thought he was to a hard, sinister character. She was actually frightened.

"Buck up your ideas, start playing nice, or things are going to get rather nasty for you. You have no idea what I am capable of and, trust me, you don't want to find out." Michael was facing her now, boring into her with cold, green eyes, and she was rooted to the spot in fear. He handed her a box of chocolates, gift wrapped with a pretty yellow bow.

"When your mother asks how we got on, you tell her you are sorry for all the petty behaviour. Tell her how much you like me and what a nice lunch we had, that I bought you these lovely chocolates. I don't want any more trouble from you, Leah. I'm serious." With that, Michael sunk his hands deep into his coat pockets, turned away and walked off, leaving Leah in stunned silence, staring after him.

When Leah got home, Anna greeted her at the door, keen to hear how things had gone. Leah pushed past her and ran up to her room, flinging the gift boxed chocolates behind her. Anna picked them up slowly, saw how nice they were and felt a pang of anger at Leah's behaviour. Michael had gone to the trouble of trying so hard with her and this was how she repaid him. She decided to let Leah stew in her own juice and got on with housework, deciding to ignore her spoilt daughter.

Meanwhile, Leah lay on her bed sobbing into her pillow. She hated Michael with a vengeance. She thought about telling her mum what he said to her today but she thought her mum would never believe her and would probably take his side. It was so frustrating. She sobbed harder now, burying her head deeper into the pillow and wishing her dad had never left.

Downstairs, Anna gave Michael a call. “Hi, how did it go today?” she asked anxiously.

“It was fine,” said Michael casually. “We had a nice chat, she apologised for being such hard work. Did she apologise to you?”

“Well, no, not exactly,” said Anna. She was confused. Leah had come home in such a furious mood yet here was Michael painting a very different picture of how the day had gone.

“That’s strange, she said she was going to apologise to you. Perhaps she will later on. How’s things with you?” Michael moved on.

They chatted amicably for a while, then made arrangements for the following evening. After the call, Anna sat on the couch for a while, the telephone still in her hands. She didn’t get it. Michael seemed upbeat and certain that Leah had been pleasant and regretful about her behaviour; but Leah had come home in a terrible mood. Maybe she was acting one way with Michael and quite another with her. It was confusing.

Anna went upstairs and knocked on Leah’s bedroom door. When she saw the state of her daughter she was taken aback. “Why are you so upset?” she asked, full of concern as she approached her daughter. She sat on the edge of her bed and smoothed down her long hair, like she used to do when she was a little girl.

"It's Michael. He called me a spoilt bitch and said I better not get on the wrong side of him, and that I didn't know what he was capable of. He scared me, Mum," Leah whimpered.

Anna was shocked. She could not imagine Michael saying those things. He was always so sweet and caring around the girls and she had seen the effort he made with them. She did not have her daughter down as a liar though, so this was all very confusing.

"Are you sure he said those exact words?" she asked, doubtfully.

"See, I knew you wouldn't believe me!" snarled Leah. "Just get out, Mum, leave me alone." She pushed her face back into the pillow, sobbing loudly.

"I'm just trying to get to the bottom of things," Anna explained. "Michael says one thing and you say another. I don't know what to believe."

"You should believe your daughter, because I'm the one telling the truth!" shouted Leah, getting hysterical. "As if he's going to admit the vile things he said. I hate him."

"Come on, don't say you hate someone, that's horrible," Anna chided. "I'll run you a nice bath and we can have some supper together. Come on, cheer up, it's not the end of the world."

Anna hated when the girls got upset. She didn't know what to think. She needed to speak to Michael again. She would be furious if he had called her daughter a bitch. Yes, she could be an obnoxious teenager, but she wasn't a bitch and she didn't want her spoken to like that.

Chapter 7

Fraud Investigation Service

Meanwhile, in Manchester, the police had had a visit from a Mr Tony Capaldi. He had some concerns about a man who had visited a gallery in which he was an investor. He had been fronting the desk that day, as the dealer had been unwell. He told the police it might be nothing; he wasn't entirely sure. He felt strongly enough about this man's visit, however, that he thought he must report it to the police.

He said the man was dressed as a priest but that during their conversation, it turned out the man knew nothing about Catholicism. It had raised his suspicions. The man was looking for the owner, hoping for a valuation on a couple of paintings he had. Although Tony did not see the paintings himself, he began to wonder at their authenticity, given the man was clearly trying to deceive him with his priest persona.

When the report landed on Detective Inspector Grant Allan's desk in London's Fraud Investigation Service, some eighteen months later, two investigators were sent to Manchester to interview Mr Capaldi. While there, they visited other galleries in the area to see if they had also had a visit from the priest.

The visit to Tony Capaldi was not enough to go on, considering the man had not even seen the paintings. However, it did seem as though something strange was going on, and

Detective Inspector Allan felt it in his bones. There was certainly more to this than met the eye and he was going to find out exactly what.

The two fraud investigators made an appointment with Tony Capaldi at his art gallery to find out what they could about the potential fraudster. He greeted them warmly and could only tell them what he had already said in his report.

"You might want to visit some of the other galleries in the area," Tony suggested helpfully. "The man was on foot, you see, and because I couldn't give him a valuation, it's highly likely he sought one from some other gallery." The two investigators thanked him for his time and set off, also on foot, looking for nearby galleries. It didn't take them long to get to the next one.

The dealer there not only remembered the priest, but confirmed he had purchased two Alfred Munnings paintings from him for a considerable amount of money. He referred to a large journal on the front desk and, sure enough, there was an entry made on the date of the visit, with the names of the paintings bought: 'Chestnuts in Bloom' and 'A Gypsy Encampment'. He had since sold them on to a Mr Lewis Thornton, who was a visitor to the area but whose address was in London.

The dealer was devastated to hear that they may have been fakes, having being so convinced by their authenticity. He was ashamed that he had not recognised them as frauds and was keen for the officers to keep him informed of updates on the investigation. The officers left with the buyer's information and decided to visit surrounding galleries, in the hope of finding out more about the mysterious priest.

The next gallery could not help but at the fourth, the dealer, who looked to be in his fifties and was wearing black-rimmed spectacles, mustard cords with a wine polo neck and a moss green cardigan, confirmed he had indeed come across the priest.

"I bought two LS Lowry paintings from him," confirmed the dealer. "Don't tell me they were fakes?" he said, his eyes downcast. "I was convinced they were the real deal."

"Why were you so convinced?" asked one of the officers, taking out his notebook.

"Lowry only ever used five colours when painting and that matched. Looking at them, I was sure it was his work. I still have them here. I was going to sell them at auction. They got so much attention I've had them up in the gallery all this time. I'll get them." The dealer walked quickly down the long corridor to the back of the building and took the paintings off the wall. Bringing them back to the officers, he stared at them hard.

"I was so convinced," he said, shaking his head disbelievingly. "See on the back these numbers," he said, pointing to the X02030 on the back of one painting and X02031 on the other. “These made me believe they must have hung together on a gallery wall at some point. That was the deciding factor for me buying them.”

“Very clever,” said the other officer, shaking his head. “Obviously that’s what he wanted you to believe. How much did you buy them for?”

“£20,000 for the pair,” the dealer admitted.

“Well, that would have been a bargain had they been the real thing,” laughed the officer.

“The priest said his church was under renovation and these were found in the attic. No-one knew where they came from or how long they had been there, so he was very pleased with that amount,” said the dealer unashamedly. “I’m glad now I didn’t offer more than that.”

“Indeed,” agreed the officer. “Unfortunately, we will have to take them with us as part of our investigation. Are you insured for these circumstances?”

“I’m not sure,” said the dealer. “I have insurance but I’m not sure it will cover this, as I really should have seen the paperwork to confirm their authenticity. I was just so convinced.”

“Ah well, a lesson learned there,” said the officer sympathetically. “Next time, make sure and get the paperwork.”

“Absolutely I will, I’m devastated and feel so stupid,” the dealer told them.

"Don't be so hard on yourself. They are excellent copies," said the officer. He and his colleague headed back to headquarters to report their findings.

∞

Back in London, Detective Inspector Allan was delighted with the investigators' findings.

"The next step will be to visit The Lowry gallery in Salford Quays and The Munnings Art Museum in Essex. We'll need to see if they keep CCTV footage going back to the times the frauds circulated. See if we can pick up anyone who resembles this priest. Good work lads," he told the investigators happily.

"We'll get on it," one of the officers replied, pleased their investigations had got off to such a good start. It would be a long shot if the museums had kept CCTV footage for that far back. Normally CCTV recordings were deleted after ninety days – but it was worth a shot.

The investigators, not surprisingly, came back empty handed. Neither gallery kept CCTV recordings for longer than ninety days, just as they had feared. It had been a long shot and they were disappointed to report back to the DI. Allan was also disappointed but not surprised. It would have been a miracle if they still had footage after all this time.

No other evidence of the priest had been reported and it

would seem he had disappeared from the scene. Perhaps he had retired, having made enough money, or maybe he had lost his nerve. It would be very difficult to find him; at least they had traced some of the fraudulent works and taken them out of circulation. That might be the best outcome they could hope for, unless he reappeared. A police report from the fraud squad had been issued to all art galleries in the UK, warning dealers and staff that reinforcing providence must be followed through when buying art, and that paperwork proving proof of purchase must be provided at all times.

In the meantime, Tony Capaldi would be brought back in to provide a composite sketch of the priest, in the hope of it appearing on *Crimewatch*. Maybe someone out there would recognise him. The public were sometimes the best help in these situations.

Chapter 8

Daniel & Jack

Daniel was making breakfast when Jack got up.

"Hey happy wanderer, how are you today?" he asked Jack, smiling despite his concern.

"What do you mean 'happy wanderer'?" asked Jack, looking confused.

"You don't remember your midnight walk last night?" asked Daniel.

"What midnight walk?" Jack was clearly baffled.

"Never mind," replied Daniel. "Here, have some breakfast. Do you want to come with me and Eve today? We're going to the Modern Art Gallery. I know you love it."

"Yes, okay," Jack said without enthusiasm, which was unusual for him. Normally a trip into Palermo to visit its galleries would fill Jack with excitement. But Daniel was pleased he agreed to join them. He didn't feel comfortable leaving him alone these days.

The men ate their breakfast, then got dressed. When Jack came out of his room, Daniel was worried to see him wearing the same trousers he'd been wearing all week, and his t-shirt was inside out.

"I think you'd better change into something fresher, and maybe put your top on the right way," he told Jack.

"What's wrong with this?" asked Jack, perplexed.

"Come on, I'll help you find something," Daniel said, pushing him back into the bedroom. He pulled out some clean linen shorts and a short-sleeved shirt and fresh underwear, just in case he hadn't been changing those either.

"Here, get changed, I'll wait for you," he said, leaving the clothes lying out on the bed. When Jack came out again, the shirt buttons were done in the wrong order.

"Come here," said Daniel impatiently. "Damn it, it's like dressing a two-year-old." Jack looked hurt and Daniel immediately regretted his impatience. "It's okay," he added. "We've got plenty of time." He was worried, though, and added these recent confusions to his list for the specialist, which was steadily getting longer.

They picked Eve up outside the hotel. She was wearing a day dress, with strappy sandals, and her black hair fell loosely down her shoulders. She looked beautiful, fresh and young. She was excited to see the gallery and didn't stop talking all the way there. Daniel laughed at her enthusiasm.

The gallery was located in a complex of the Church of St'Anna la Misericordia, in the historic centre of the city. The peaceful building held an array of impressive modern art from the 19th and 20th centuries, and housed both paintings and sculptures. The trio were delighted to check out Leonardo da Vinci's very technical exhibition and spent a great deal of time observing the artist's skills and perceptions. It made Daniel miss his art tremendously. Since living down here he had done very little in the way of painting. It was a waste having so much natural beauty around him. He vowed to pick it up again soon. The gallery had three floors and Jack excused himself; he wanted to wander off by himself, quietly taking in the beauty around him.

Daniel and Eve followed discreetly, a clear length away from him, and Daniel shared his concerns for the old man. He told Eve of Jack's recent memory loss, the problems he'd had dressing that morning, his poor concentration and, most recently, his bizarre walk in the middle of the night. She could see he was deeply concerned for him and it moved her.

"Have you been to see a professional?" she asked.

"We have an appointment for next week," Daniel told her. "I want a diagnosis but at the same time I am afraid of what they are going to tell us. I'm sure it won't be good and what do I do? Do I tell Jack or do I carry on like nothing's happening? It's getting to the stage where I am afraid to leave him on his own and, to be honest, I don't want to spend another winter here. I want to move on."

Daniel surprised himself. He hadn't realised until that moment that he wanted to get away from Mondello and start living a more normal life, in a place where everyone spoke

English and where he could find work, maybe in art. The idea of teaching art had appealed to him.

"You looked surprised when you said that," Eve said perceptively.

"I guess I am," he replied. "I never planned to stay here forever. Now, with Jack's health failing, I'm afraid I won't be able to leave. I need to make sure he is okay. He's like a father to me now."

"At the same time, you can't put your life on hold to care for him," Eve said wisely. "Maybe he'll need more professional care once you receive a diagnosis."

"Oh, it's depressing," said Daniel, shaking his head. He watched Jack stopping at different exhibitions, staring at them thoughtfully, lost in their beauty.

"You never said how the two of you became so close," Eve said, joining Daniel to sit on a bench, where they could still keep an eye on Jack.

Daniel thought about telling Eve about the art frauds and wondered how she would take it. Would she see him in a different light? It was a gamble. He felt good after telling her about his past the night before; maybe this would help unburden him of some of his doubts about himself. He figured he had nothing to lose.

Daniel told Eve about the failed robbery at Jack's place and how they duped Reggie into returning. He explained how he was then obligated into helping Jack, with his plans for the fraudulent paintings.

Eve's jaw had dropped during this monologue. "You have been the victim of circumstance so many times," she said. "This is unbelievable. Were you not terrified of getting caught?"

"We both were, of course," admitted Daniel. "But I didn't have that much to lose any more. There was an element of who dares wins, a sense of unreality about the whole thing; I just went along with it.

"When Jack was nearly rumbled due to his ignorance of the Jesuit order, he decided to hang up the old priest routine and retire down here in Mondello. I had several paintings left that I had worked hard on and I didn't want to leave without making sure Anna and the girls were financially sound. After all, that is the only thing I can do for them since I am no longer part of their lives.

"But when I was in London I came across Reggie again. He threatened to expose me. I felt sick to my stomach, suffocated, I needed to be free of him forever. I followed him and when he reached a crossing, I… I pushed him in front of a bus. He died, Eve. I killed him and for that I will always be sorry. It is the biggest regret in my life. But I felt like the man would never leave me in peace. He would always be there to ruin any good thing that came my way.

"Reggie had attacked my wife and I could never forgive him for that."

He looked at Eve to gauge her reaction. She was silent and looked ashen.

"You hate me now. I know I'm a monster, a terrible person, a murderer. How could I ever redeem myself in this life? I can't, Eve, that's the sad fact. No-one could hate me more than I hate myself."

Jack rejoined them and the conversation came to an awkward halt.

"Gareth, where the hell have you been?" Jack suddenly raged at Daniel. "You never even came to your mother's funeral. You are dead to me." Daniel calmed him down and sat him down on the bench next to Eve.

"Jack, it's me, I'm not Gareth. It's okay, calm down." Daniel was drained having just confessed all to Eve. Now Jack was acting all crazy again, he needed to get out of there.

"Steve," said Jack, coming around and thankfully remembering his false name. Although, Daniel thought, the way he had been acting, it wouldn't matter if he mistakenly called him by his real name. Everything he said was confusing.

"I'm tired, I want to go back to the villa," said Jack, shakily.

"I think that's a good idea," said Daniel. "I'm sorry, Eve,

to cut the day short. Do you want to come back, too? I'll make us some lunch."

"That's okay, Steve. If you don't mind I'd rather stay and visit a few more places while I'm here." Eve's voice was distant, and she wouldn't look at him. Daniel prayed he hadn't put her off him, frightened her away. He felt sick to his stomach.

"Can I take you out this evening?" he pressed, trying to read her.

"See how Jack is, then maybe give me a call," she answered non-committally.

"Sure," answered Daniel unhappily. "Call you later then."

∞

On the drive home, Daniel fretted about all he had told Eve. Maybe he had been wrong to trust her. She could quite easily go to the police. He didn't think she would but he realised he hardly knew the girl. He had been careless telling her so much.

Back at the villa, he made him and Jack a light lunch, then Jack went for a sleep. Daniel swam length after length in the pool, trying to wash away the morning's events.

Chapter 9

Anna

The girls were at their friends' houses, and Anna invited Michael for a meal. She hoped to get to the bottom of what really happened during his day out with Leah. Her daughter had said nothing else on the subject but had remained moody and down. Michael arrived looking devastatingly handsome, as usual. She greeted him with a kiss and a hug and breathed in his heady aroma. He always smelled so expensive; she momentarily forgot she was mad at him, if he had indeed called her daughter a bitch.

After they had eaten supper they were seated on the couch with a glass of wine, cosy and relaxed in each other's company. Anna chose that moment to broach the subject of Leah.

"So, your day with Leah," she began smoothly. "How did it really go?"

"I told you already," said Michael impatiently. "She was apologetic about the way she behaved. She said she would apologise to you, too. We had lunch, I bought her chocolates and when she left she even gave me a warm hug."

"That's so strange, because when she came home she was in a furious mood. She went straight to her room, crying. She said you called her a spoilt bitch, Michael. Is that true?" Anna felt strangely bad asking him but she had to know the truth.

Michael, looking horrified, took her hands in his and

looked her straight in the eye. "Do you really think I did that?" he asked. He was the picture of innocence. She shook her head, and smiled with relief.

"No, I really don't think you did," she admitted. "I had to ask, Michael. I just don't know what's going on in her head right now. She's even started talking about wanting to see her father again."

"Really?" asked Michael, eyes wide. "You never really told me what happened with you and their father. Do you still have contact with him?"

"Well, I told you about him hitting the bottle. He lost his job, we moved in with Susan. He was horrible to be around and had changed so much, in such a short time," Anna hesitated. She wasn't sure whether to tell him about being attacked; she felt she had to. It would explain her reluctance to take the relationship that one step further. Memories of that awful night still consumed her and she felt it difficult to go there, even with Michael, who she adored. "I didn't tell you the next part," she said, hanging her head in shame. Then the words tumbled from her. "I was out with Rachel and Susan one evening. We got really drunk, let our hair down, I met a man, he flattered me with attention and said all the right things. He took me outside and..." she hesitated, unwilling to go on.

"And?" said Michael gently.

"And he attacked me. I didn't tell Daniel. Somehow he found out. It turned out he knew this man. It was someone from his past who was seeking revenge. I went to the police to prove to Daniel that I had been attacked. It was too late for us, the marriage was over. He could not look at me and I know he blamed me for what happened."

She began sobbing quietly now. The memory was still so painful. Michael held her in his arms until the sobbing subsided.

"It wasn't your fault," he told her firmly. "It's okay, Anna, you are safe with me. Why did the man want revenge on Daniel, though?"

"I honestly don't know," said Anna. Her head felt muddy and she didn't want to say anything else about Daniel or Reggie. "Let's just cuddle and not talk any more tonight," pleaded Anna.

"Sure," agreed Michael, but his mind was racing as she snuggled him closely.

Chapter 10

The Browns (two years ago)

When Reggie's father answered the knock at the door one Friday morning, he was still mourning the death of his beloved wife. He was shocked to see two police officers on the doorstep, sympathetic looks on their faces.

"Can we come in?" asked one of the officers, walking in anyway.

When the police had searched the flat Reggie rented in Soho, they found his army documents and discharge notice, with his dad listed as next of kin.

"What's all this about?" asked Frank, following them and indicating they should go into the living room, where they sat down.

"Do you have a son, Reggie Raymond Brown?" the officer asked.

"Yes. But I've not seen him for years." Frank's face was a picture of confusion and worry.

"I'm sorry to tell you, your son has been killed. He was pushed in front of a bus in London yesterday." The police officer watched Frank's face drain of colour. He gripped the side of the chair as the room spun. He had remained angry and upset at Reggie for stealing from their friends, at his own aunt's funeral, but had always hoped he would see him again and they would be reconciled.

"What do you mean pushed?" asked Frank. "Do you mean he was murdered?"

"It would seem so," confirmed the officer. "However, we do not know by whom or why."

"Are you investigating?" asked Frank, his voice growing louder with emotion. "I want the person who killed my son brought to justice."

"An investigation is underway. There will be a duty officer appointed to you and your family to keep you abreast of developments and also offer any support they can. Is there anyone we can call, to be with you right now? It's been a shock for you I'm sure."

"Yes, call my son Thomas, tell him to come down right away."

When Tommy arrived, Frank was alone, still in the same seat. He had been pinned to the spot by this new knowledge. His youngest son had been murdered.

"Dad, what's happened?" asked Tommy, kneeling down beside his father. The family were still coming to terms with their mother's death and Tommy was disturbed by the broken expression on his dad's face.

"It's our Reggie. He's been killed. Murdered they said, pushed in front of a bus in London. They don't know who or why, but by God we are going to find out, son. You need to sort this," Frank grabbed his eldest son's arm tightly. His face was white and his eyes full of sadness and regret.

"He was only a petty thief," he continued, grief stricken. "He didn't need to stay away all those years. I would've forgiven him, moved past it. I always thought I'd have the chance to see him again. Now I never will." He sobbed uncontrollably then, an explosion of grief for his wife and now for his youngest son, who lay cold in a morgue somewhere in London.

Tommy would have to go and identify the body. He held his father firmly, his handsome features set in stone, his whole body tightened up. He would get revenge for his brother, if it was the last thing he ever did. He wasn't surprised to hear he had been murdered. He always knew Reggie was a bad apple and he always knew he'd come to a sticky end. He was, however, furious that someone thought it was okay to kill his brother, without fear of reprisals. He would make sure there were reprisals.

∞

When Tommy met Cassandra, she almost immediately confided that she was prone to bouts of depression. He didn't know where it stemmed from and he didn't think even Cassandra knew. It was just something in her make up. He naively thought his love would be enough to make her happy. They married, he bought her a beautiful house. She always wanted kids and they had two, a boy and a girl.

Through the years, though, her depression got worse. When she became disinterested and dangerous for the kids to be around, when she nearly burned the house down one night by falling asleep with a cigarette in her hand, Tommy had had enough. He unceremoniously packed her belongings and dumped her at her sister's in Manchester. He did not want to see her again. The kids were eight and ten and Tommy decided they would be better off without their mother.

Tommy started his working life in the used car business. He would buy used cars, do them up a treat and sell them for a decent profit. Since then, he had escalated his business to premier cars and did a bit of dodgy dealing on the side, getting rid of stolen property. Though he never took part in any robberies himself, he was happy to be the middle man and found it very profitable. He was always very careful who he did business with, though, and so far remained unknown to the law.

When his sister Denise's boyfriend Gino turned out to be a drug-selling pimp who left her for dead after a brutal beating, Tommy hired the talents of private detective Rob Imrie to locate him. It didn't take Rob long and Tommy picked Gino up soon after. He took him deep into the woods and made him inject heroin into any veins he had left, standing over him to see it done. Gino knew this was a better way to go than what Tommy could and should do to him, accepting his fate and welcoming oblivion when it came.

When Gino's body was found, it was recorded as a drug overdose and the police were not sorry to see the back of him. It was an open and shut case, no investigations were carried out and no-one mourned for him – least of all Denise. She happily remarried and was expecting her third child. She never knew about Tommy's involvement in Gino's death. No-one did.

Tommy called Rob Imrie – his talents were needed again, this time to find out what had happened to his brother. He would deal with the rest.

∞

Tommy's daughter Eve had grown up to be a beautiful young lady. Long shiny black hair, huge brown eyes and a great figure. She had shown an interest in the fashion world and was currently studying for a degree. His son Michael was helping Tommy in the family business and was showing great signs of being a real gem in the selling of stolen goods. He was a great asset to Tommy, who was proud of both his children and treasured them above all else in this world. They were his best friends, as well as his children.

Chapter 11

Rob Imrie (two years ago)

Rob Imrie had his work cut out. The call from Tommy did not rattle him. He was good at what he did and he would find out what happened to Reggie. He had contacts everywhere: in the police and the criminal world. He could get information from useful sources. He scanned the army papers Tommy had emailed him.

Reggie had a good record as a serviceman but had been discharged on medical grounds. He saw the signing officer's name: Jack Blair. He made a note of this and thought he might need to speak to him at some point. For now, he was in the streets of London, where the homeless and down-and-outs hung out. He knew that Reggie had run way from home, and that not a lot of effort had been made to find him.

Tommy said he had wanted to see how the little runt survived.

But a witness had seen Reggie board a train at about 1pm all those years ago. Rob went to the station to see which trains left at 1pm and what their destinations were.

The train Reggie got was probably London bound. There were plenty stops in between. In Rob's experience, runaways normally took their preferred mode of transport to the furthest point away from their home town. Reggie had no doubt spent time on the streets, and Rob wanted to see if anyone remembered him. It didn't take much to get information from a desperate person. A cup of coffee and some hot food usually did the trick.

After talking to around twenty homeless people, Rob got lucky. A small woman with dirty blonde, wiry hair who looked to be in her forties, but was probably only in her thirties, remembered Reggie. Rob bought her a fish supper. They sat on a bench together while she hungrily tucked in.

"I remember Reggie," she said, munching on a chip smothered with tomato sauce. Some dribbled down her dirty chin. Rob looked away in disgust.

"What do you remember about him?" fished Rob. He was tired and now impatient.

"He was always going on about wanting revenge. He was a soldier, you see," she said, looking pleased with herself.

"Yes, I already know that," said Rob, not sorry to burst her bubble.

"Well, he had been in a coma. He said something about another soldier being a coward. He told me the whole story but I never really listened much. I remember the other soldier's name was Daniel, though. He repeated that name often enough. Oh, and he wanted revenge on his superior. I think his name was Mac or maybe Jack. Yeah, Jack – it was Jack. He got him kicked out of the army, you see, he said Reggie was medically unfit," and the woman smiled broadly. "I told him life's too short for revenge and better just forgetting it. Then he got angry with me so I just dropped the subject. He was mean when he was angry. I was glad he didn't want revenge on me for anything, put it that way," she said, suddenly looking fearful.

"Is there anything else you remember? Did he say where he was going to find these men?" asked Rob, hopefully.

"He said Yorkshire, I think. I'm not a hundred percent sure," she said, and shrugged. "That's all I can really tell you about Reggie. He was a handsome lad, down on his luck but he was kind to me. Shared food and smokes. Only, I didn't like being around him when he got mad," she shook her head. Rob slipped her thirty quid and went on his way. His next step would be to the barracks to speak to soldiers who served with Reggie in Afghanistan.

Some of the men agreed to talk with him.

"So, can anyone tell me what happened to Reggie? How did he end up in a coma?" Rob got straight to the point.

"Aye, he was shot up during a village raid," offered a red-haired soldier with a broad Glaswegian accent. "Four of the men he was with were killed. Daniel Edgar was uninjured. Apparently he froze upstairs, so Reggie says. He got voluntary discharge after that whole episode, couldnae hack it after that."

"That's right," added another soldier thoughtfully. "Reggie

said Daniel was a coward that night. No-one could prove that at the inquest because he was the only one fit to give evidence."

"What was Reggie like after the incident?" asked Rob.

"He was away wi' it," said the Scotsman. "Aff his nut. He would fly aff the handle at the slightest thing and naebody liked being around him. Aye, the man was a loose cannon."

"Commanding Officer Blair insisted he be medically discharged, and he was raging at that," added another. "Suffered from PTSD, he did. Everyone was relieved when he went, to be honest."

"It was a shame, he had been a good serviceman though," piped up another voice. "He told the Commanding Officer he would get his revenge. Don't know if he did or not. I think Jack Blair retired, heard he was in Yorkshire now."

"Well, thanks lads, that's been really helpful," concluded Rob, and he meant it.

"Nae bother, big man," said the Scotsman. "I'll see you after."

On the way out, Rob got a call from his source in the police. He was told that Daniel Edgar was under suspicion for pushing Reggie Raymond Brown in front of a bus in London. He had gone off the radar and no-one knew his whereabouts. It was suspected he was no longer in the country and could be anywhere. His wife and children still resided in Yorkshire; he passed on the address, which Rob carefully noted down. That was twice within the hour he had heard the name Daniel Edgar.

His next move was to find out more about Jack Blair and see if there was a connection. He found out he had a farmhouse and took a trip there. When he arrived he could see kids playing out the back and a lady hanging out washing. This didn't look like the place of a retired serviceman.

"Hi," he said, approaching the lady. "Sorry to bother you. I was looking for Jack Blair."

"Jack? Oh, he was the previous owner. Doesn't live here now," she said, continuing to hang her washing.

"Any idea where he moved on to?" he asked.

"Sorry, no idea," she answered as she pegged up a shirt. Rob drove into the nearest village and went to the first newsagent he saw. He picked up a newspaper and took it to the counter.

"Lovely day," he said conversationally.

"Yes, indeed it is," answered the man behind the counter.

"Had this place long?" aked Rob.

"Over twenty years," said the man proudly.

"I'll bet you know everyone around here then," Rob said, smiling.

"And their dogs," answered the man, laughing.

"You wouldn't know Jack Blair? Lived in the old farmhouse up the road?" he asked. "We were old comrades and I thought I'd drop in on him, only to find he's moved on somewhere."

"Jack's not there any more," the shopkeeper said, stating the obvious. "He told me the day he left he was off to Italy to retire. Said he would never be back. Where was it now? A place with galleries. He loved art. It began with 'P'. Plamo… no, that wasn't it. Something like that, though," he said, seeming frustrated.

"Palermo," stated Rob.

"That's it! Said something about finding a beach down there to set up home. Oh dear, I just remembered he said not to tell anyone. I don't know why but sure, if you're an old friend, I'm sure it's okay I've told you," he said, unconvincingly.

"It's fine, think nothing of it, it's not like I'm going to Palermo for a catch up," laughed Rob, delighted to have found this out. Tommy would be pleased. "Was he going alone?" Rob probed.

"Yes, I think so. I think he had someone staying with him for a while, because he was buying more food than usual. More than you'd need for one – but I really don't know. He certainly never said he was going with anyone else."

"I see. Just wondered. One of my old mates from the army said he was going to look him up. I wondered if he'd managed, that's all."

"Sorry, I really couldn't confirm that," said the shopkeeper, annoyed he couldn't help further. He was enjoying being the source of so much information.

"No, don't worry about it," Rob said, paying for the paper. "Take care," he added as he left the shop.

He placed a call to Tommy to report back all he had learned.

"Great job, Rob. I knew I could count on you. I'll take it from here," Tommy told him. He had more than enough information now to set his plans in motion.

Chapter 12

Leah

At her friend Claire's house, Leah poured her heart out about how much she hated Michael. "My mum's oblivious to how nasty he can be," she complained bitterly. "He acts all nice in front of her, but when we are alone he's horrible. It's so frustrating. She won't believe me," she despaired.

"Why don't you record him on your phone?" Claire suggested. "That way you can show your mum and she will have no choice but to believe you."

"He would know," said Leah, thinking it through.

"Not if you hid it among books or on top of your dresser or something," said Claire.

"I don't know, he'd go mental if he found it," said Leah, looking anxious.

"He won't, though, not if you conceal it properly. Maybe even in your wardrobe with the door open," Claire persisted.

"Yes, I could do that," said Leah, brightening up a bit. "I'd have to be really careful, but I think that could work. Thanks Claire, you're such a good friend. I'm so glad I've got you to let off steam to. Sometimes I feel like I'm going mad. I miss my dad so much. I really want to see him."

"Yeah, it must be tough not having him around," Claire sympathised. "Hey, do you fancy some snacks and a movie to take your mind off it all?"

"Sure do," said Leah, forgetting all about her problems with Michael, for the moment.

When she got home she looked around her room for places she could hide her phone. Michael was coming round for tea again tonight. If he dared come up to her room and threaten her, she was going to catch him at it. There were shelves in her built-in wardrobe – she could easily stand the phone on one of the shelves. It should show most of the room and whoever was in it. She would place it here if she needed to. Happy with that, she pulled out her homework and got down to some studying.

Still in her room, she heard the door open and close, heralding the arrival of Michael. She cringed when she heard his voice, all sweetness and light for her mum. She could hear Anna's happy tones and then plates being laid out in the kitchen.

"Leah, tea's out!" shouted Anna.

"Coming," Leah replied grumpily, wishing she were anywhere else.

Michael had brought a Chinese for a treat. Eloise was already at the table grinning stupidly and smiling lovingly at Michael. Leah felt like shaking her but just sat down next to her.

"Look what Michael brought us for a nice treat," said Anna, sweeping her arm over the Chinese food like it was gold dust. "What do you say, then?" she asked.

“Thank you, Michael,” the girls said in unison.

“My pleasure,” said Michael, carrying out a dramatic bow. “All I ask in return is that you enjoy. Is that okay with you, Princess Leah?” he mocked.

“I suppose,” Leah managed without looking at him. But when Michael sat opposite her and she realised she would have to look at him at some point, she wanted the ground to open up and swallow her.

They began eating. Leah realised she could spend no more time in the same room as Michael, and picked up her plate to leave the table.

“Leah, where do you think you’re going?” Anna snapped.

“Up to my room to eat, I need to finish my homework.” Leah said quietly.

“Sit back down this minute, you can finish it after your meal,” Anna ordered.

“But Mum, I don’t want to,” Leah replied, looking miserable.

“Do as your mother says and sit down,” said Michael, looking at her coldly.

“You’re not my dad!” shouted Leah in frustration, slamming the plate down so the food splattered all over the unit. She ran from the kitchen, slamming the door behind her.

“Leah!” shouted Anna, cheeks flushed with

embarrassment. She got up to go after her daughter but Michael stood up immediately.

"Don't, I'll go. You sit and finish your food." Anna looked unsure. "It's okay, I'll be gentle," he said, laughing, "I'll have her back here in a jiffy."

"Okay," she said, gratefully. "I'm so sorry Michael, she's acting terribly."

"She's just a teenager," reasoned Michael. "That's what teenagers do."

He climbed the stairs at top speed and was in Leah's room before she'd even heard him. But in anticipation of him following her, she had quickly pressed the record button on her phone and set it down on the shelf in her wardrobe, making out like she was getting a jumper.

"Hey," he said softly. "Are you okay?" He looked genuinely concerned and his change in demeanour confused her. "I'm sorry if I came across like a dad. I know I'm not your dad and I would never want to replace him," he said gently. "Can you please come down and finish your meal. Your mum's upset and this can all be sorted if you would just come down. Then you can disappear the entire night and not have to look at my ugly face," he said, laughing. He was being so nice, for a minute Leah thought he meant it.

Then he reached into the wardrobe and took the phone off

the shelf.

"Don't forget your phone," he said, hitting the record button. "Do you think I'm bloody stupid?" His handsome features turned ugly and threatening. "Get your spoilt little butt back downstairs this minute or I'll teach you a lesson you'll never forget."

Terrified, Leah grabbed her phone and ran back downstairs to the safety of her mother. She sat down and ate her meal without speaking another word. Michael re-entered the room smiling at Anna, and giving her a little wink.

"Who fancies the cinema this weekend?" he asked, smiling broadly.

"Me!" screamed Eloise excitedly. "I love the movies!"

"Me too," said Michael, getting up to give the little girl a hug. Anna smiled at them while Leah looked down at the table. She was white as a sheet. She could never win.

Chapter 13

Eve

In her hotel room, Eve called her father. "Dad, it's me," she said down the receiver. "I didn't know what an awful person my uncle was."

"What?" asked Tommy. "What are you talking about?"

"Daniel's been telling me all about your little brother. From what he told me, he sounds like a disgusting human being," she answered.

"It doesn't matter what he was like," Tommy told her. "He was my brother and that man murdered him. Don't forget that, Eve."

"With good reason," answered Eve, assertively. "What he did to Daniel, anyone would have murdered him in those circumstances."

"Don't be going all soft on me, Eve," Tommy warned. "It sounds like you're getting a little too fond of your sailor boy."

"No I'm not," she protested. "I'm just trying to figure out what we are doing here. What is it you want from Daniel? He's not the evil man you make him out to be."

"He killed my brother, Eve," Tommy sighed heavily. "I cannot let him get away with it. He's got away with it for long enough already. You have done a brilliant job getting to know him. You've done everything I've asked – thank you. Maybe it's time you went home. I can take it from here."

"Take what from here? What are you going to do?" Eve asked, holding her breath.

"That's for me to know," said Tommy. Eve could tell by the tone of his voice it would be unwise to question him any further, so she changed tack.

"Sure Dad, you know what's best. Can I stay another few days, though? I love it down here and I wanted to visit some boutiques in Palermo to see what fabrics and styles they use, to help with my coursework."

"We'll see," said Tommy. "Listen angel, please don't get involved in things that don't concern you. You do your own thing now, don't see Daniel again unless I need you to, understand?"

"Yes of course, thanks Dad," she said, replacing the receiver. She sat for a few minutes, deep in thought. She was worried for Daniel and what her father might do to him. She knew her dad could be a violent man and she guessed whatever he was planning would not be pretty.

Meanwhile, Michael was video calling his dad in Italy. "Hey holiday maker, how's it going?" he asked.

"All's going well this end. How about you?" Tommy asked.

"Yep, all in place here, too. I've got the lovely ex-wife falling at my feet and the youngest loves me, too. Leah, the oldest kid, is the only fly in the ointment. She's hankering after seeing her old dad again."

"Well, is she now? That might just fit in with my plans, son," said Tommy, thinking hard. "Tell you what, why don't you encourage them to come down? Make it within the next couple of weeks if you can."

"Sounds good, Dad. I'll try my best – it'd be good to get some sunshine," Michael replied, his face lighting up at the thought of it.

Tommy broke out into a sinister smile. This might just fit into his plan for revenge. It would be a lot cleaner than what he had originally planned. If they were all here together, it would be a lot tidier. He could tie up all the loose ends and he and his family could go home and get on with their lives.

Chapter 14

Daniel & Jack

Daniel called Eve at the hotel to see if she fancied dinner.

"Hi, it's Steve," he said breezily down the phone. She thought it was amazing how Jack and Daniel kept remembering to call him Steve. The family had found out through the private detective that this was a name he had used since fleeing Canada. Even Jack, with his health problems, had never once slipped up and called him Daniel.

"Hi," said Eve flatly.

"I wondered if you were bored. Would you like to join me for dinner tonight?" he asked.

"I'm okay tonight, thanks Steve. I've ordered room service and was just going to stay and do some studying for my coursework."

"Oh okay," he answered, sounding disappointed. "Listen, I hope what I shared with you has not put you off me, or made you think less of me. I see you as such a good friend and your opinion of me really matters. It was unfair of me to lay that on you, it was a lot. I can understand why you might not want to see me, it was selfish. It just felt so good to unburden myself with some things from the past," he said, honestly. Eve felt bad for him. She wanted more than anything to go for dinner but her dad had warned her not to see him again – and she knew better than to disobey him.

"I don't think any less of you," she said, quietly. "I think anyone in your circumstances would have done the same thing. From what you've told me, you have been the victim of circumstances your entire life. I really hope that in the future you are free from all those demons. Even Jack… I know he's your friend now but he has led you down a criminal path, Steve. Is that really friendship? Holding you over a barrel to do what you did. I know you see him as a father figure now, but don't let him hold you back. If you can, get away from here, from him and start a new life. The life you've always wanted. It's not too late."

It had suddenly occurred to Eve that it might be a good idea to get Daniel to leave, so that her father could not hurt him.

"Thank you so much, Eve," Daniel replied, relieved. "You don't know how much it means to me. I've been so worried you thought I was a monster. You've no idea. I know Jack blackmailed me, in a way, to carry out the frauds. But I could have walked away. I don't think he would have carried out his threats of going to the police. He was just a bored, lonely old man and he actually has become a good friend. I can't leave until I know Jack is going to be alright. I'll stay as long as he needs me."

That was not what Eve wanted to hear. She wanted Daniel far away from her father. She would need to think of something but for now she was at a loss. "I understand," she said, not understanding. "I'll speak to you soon, Steve," she said, ending the call. She needed time to think of a plan.

∞

Daniel checked over the list of things he had noticed about Jack's behaviour, ready to take to the specialist. His stomach was in knots. He was feeling anxious about the outcome of the visit and couldn't help but fear the worst. As they drove to the hospital Jack was very quiet. He had argued with Daniel about going. "There's nothing wrong with me," he had insisted.

"You've not been yourself for a while now," Daniel said, softly. "Forgetting things, calling me Gareth all the time."

"Have I?" asked Jack, looking confused, "I don't remember that."

"Yes, you call me Gareth quite a lot," said Daniel.

"Well, I don't know why I'd do that. I've not seen my son in years," said Jack, looking out of the window.

"It's not just that Jack; it's getting up in the middle of the night, wandering off," Daniel told him. By the time they got out the car, Jack was agitated and wanted to go home. "Come on, it'll be fine," Daniel cajoled him.

After a short time in the waiting area, a tall man with thinning hair popped his head round the door.

"Can I see Mr Blair now, please?" he called.

"Come on, that's us," said Daniel, pulling Jack to his feet.

They followed the man to a consulting room, where he turned round to shake their hands.

"Hi, I'm Dr Romano," he said, indicating they should take a seat. "So, can you tell me a little bit about what has been going on? I see from Dr Rossi's report that Jack has been suffering confusion and forgetfulness."

"I'm fine, doctor, really," Jack said, smiling.

"Jack has been forgetting a lot," interrupted Daniel. "He goes in and out of rooms forgetting what he came in for. He got dressed in the middle of the night and went to buy breakfast rolls. Luckily I found him down the street before he came to any harm. He's flooded the bathroom on more than one occasion, forgetting he was running a bath. He calls me by his son's name. He has taken a liking to strange food combinations."

"Such as?" asked the doctor, looking interested.

"Well, the other morning he put a poached egg on toast he had already spread with marmalade," said Daniel, raising one eyebrow. "Also, he does not seem to follow plot lines well when watching TV or a movie. He always loved going out, socialising, but now he seems to be tired much of the time and is not keen to go to the usual places. Do the usual things."

"I see," said the doctor, looking down as he wrote some notes. "I think I would like Jack to stay with us today, perhaps overnight. I need to carry out a series of cognitive and neurological tests to be able to make an assessment. I would also like to carry out a brain scan, to get a closer look at Jack's brain and how it is working. This can help rule out other problems, like bleeding, a stroke or a brain tumour."

"Okay, that's fine," said Daniel, "I'll go home and pack an overnight bag and bring it in. You'll be okay Jack, the doctor just wants to run some tests."

"I know," answered Jack curtly, "I'm not stupid, I heard what the man said."

The doctor showed Daniel to the door. "Don't worry," he told Daniel. "He is in good hands."

"Thank you, Dr Romano," said Daniel, shaking his hand firmly. He was confident they would find an answer to Jack's declining health.

Chapter 15

Anna

Leah had been quiet all week. Anna was worried about her.

"You okay, hun?" she asked.

"Yeah, I've just been thinking a lot about Dad lately," Leah told Anna. "Would we be able to go see him at some point?"

"I'm not sure if that's possible," Anna replied.

"Why?" shot back Leah. "Does he not want to see us?"

"Of course he wants to see you. It's not that. I can't just jump on a plane to Italy at the drop of a hat. Your dad might be busy, too. I'd have to think it over." Anna's heart was hammering at the thought of seeing Daniel again. She didn't give him much thought but now that Leah was insisting on seeing him, she had very little choice but to think about him. She decided she would talk it over with Michael. Then she would have to call Daniel from Susan's house and see what he thought about the idea of them all going over. Maybe it would do Leah good to spend some time with her father, get away from it all for a while. She might have a closer bond with Michael if he chose to come with them.

"I just don't know what to do for the best," she told Michael later that night, having told him of Leah's desire to see her father.

"Maybe you should indulge her," Michael suggested.

"Do you really think so?" asked Anna.

"Yes, why not. When's the last time they saw their dad?"

"A good few years ago now," Anna admitted.

"Well then, the man would probably love to see his kids, too. It's a win win situation," said Michael, clapping his hands together.

"Would you come, too?" Anna asked gingerly.

"Would you want me to?" asked Michael.

"Of course I'd want you to," said Anna, hugging him close. "You're the best, Michael. When I tell Leah you are supporting her on this, I can't see how she could not love you for it."

"Oh, I'm not sure anything I do could make her love me – or even like me," he said sadly. "I really try my best, you know?"

"I know you do. No-one could try harder than you, my love," Anna answered, squeezing him tight again. "I'll just have to contact Daniel now to see if it suits him – something I'm not looking forward to. You never know, he might put a kibosh on the whole thing. I better speak to him first before getting Leah's hopes up."

They spent the rest of the night watching a movie. Anna could not concentrate, her mind wandering to the conversation she would need to have with Daniel. She didn't look forward to it.

∞

The next day she went round to Susan's house. Susan made coffee while Anna told her of her plans to go and visit Daniel in Italy.

"Leah is desperate to see him. For some reason she doesn't like Michael. He's so good to her, too, bends over backwards to try and please her. She's so difficult with him. It makes things so awkward. Otherwise things are going great with him," Anna told her.

"That's not like her," replied Susan, thoughtfully. "She's normally so easy-going. Do you think she's feeling threatened by Michael and maybe thinking she's losing you a bit?"

"Maybe," said Anna. "Although, I don't know how. I still put the girls first always and we are careful not to be too affectionate with each other when they are around. I was quite shocked when she mentioned seeing Daniel. We haven't really talked about him much."

"How are you feeling about seeing him again?" asked Susan, handing her a coffee.

"Very apprehensive," Anna admitted. "It's like when you are seeing someone and you break up; I mean, do you ever want to see that person again? No. If I had my way I would never see him again. It's difficult because he is the girls' father and they have every right to see him. I know he would love to see them.

Why is life so hard sometimes?"

"It might be a good thing," Susan soothed. "You never know, maybe the break will do you all good and bring you all closer together. Do you want to ring him now?"

"Yeah, may as well get this over and done with," answered Anna.

She went into the lounge to call Daniel. When he answered the phone and heard her voice, Daniel was clearly shocked. "Are you okay? Is anything wrong? Are the girls okay?"

"Yes, we are all fine, it's okay, calm down. I'm ringing because Leah has been asking for you. She has expressed her wish to come and see you," Anna told him, half hoping he would say it was a ridiculous idea.

"Really?" asked Daniel, sounding incredulous.

"Yes, really. Do you think a visit would be possible?" she asked.

"A visit would be wonderful," he answered, excitedly. "Just Leah or all three of you?"

"Well, actually it would be four of us. I've met someone, Daniel. It's still fairly early days, but I would like him to join us, if you're okay with that?"

The line went silent and Anna counted the seconds that passed before Daniel answered. "Sure, yes, of course, it's fine," he finally said. "When are you coming? I'll get some rooms ready here at the villa."

"We don't have to stay with you, Daniel. We can book a hotel," Anna said quickly. She couldn't face staying with her estranged husband, especially with Michael on the scene.

"Don't be silly, Anna, there's plenty room here for personal space. Think it over and let me know. Honestly, the place is so big it won't be a problem. I just want to spend every minute I can with the girls. They are never out my mind," he persisted.

"Okay, I'll discuss it with Michael and see what he thinks," she said, the words out of her mouth before she realised how hurt Daniel would be.

"Okay, do that," he said shortly. Then he added, more softly, "Just get them here."

"I'll call you again when I've booked the flights and let you know when we're coming," Anna said, and replaced the receiver.

She sat quietly for a bit. It was strange talking to Daniel again. He certainly seemed keen for them to go and he didn't seem too upset that she was bringing someone. Maybe it wouldn't be as awkward as she'd first thought. Maybe he was in a relationship now – she should have asked. She was excited to get home now to break the news to the girls. Especially Leah. She would be over the moon.

Chapter 16

Daniel & Jack

Daniel sat on the couch, still clutching the phone in his hands. He couldn't believe it. His girls were coming to visit him. He was ecstatic. He had been thinking of them a lot recently and didn't know when he would get a chance to see them again.

Daniel could hardly believe they would want to see him again. It was like a dream come true. He got up and went quickly around the villa, envisaging where everyone could sleep. There was a double bedroom with en suite at the back of the accommodation, which would suit Anna and her new boyfriend. Further up the corridor were numerous rooms of different sizes; the girls could take their pick. In any case, he would prepare two of the best rooms for them and make sure they were kitted out with everything they could wish for: TVs, laptops, games consoles, mini fridges packed with goodies, the best cotton sheets. He planned to give them money to buy whatever they wanted at the many boutiques in Palermo.

He had a lot of making up to do and he could not wait to do it. When the phone rang, he ran to it, thinking it might be Anna again.

"Hello," he answered in high spirits.

"Hello, is that Steve Arnold?" asked a familiar voice.

"Yes, this is he," he answered, his mood suddenly swooping.

"It's Dr Romano – can you come to the hospital? I'd like to discuss Jack's diagnosis with you." He sounded serious and Daniel's heart sunk.

"Sure. I can be there within the hour." Daniel hung up the phone and stood staring at it for a moment.

∞

"Come in, please take a seat." Dr Romano welcomed Daniel into the room. "I wanted to discuss Jack with you alone, before having a chat with him. I believe you are listed as his next of kin."

"He has a son he hasn't seen or spoken to for years, so I guess I am his next of kin," confirmed Daniel.

Dr Romano shuffled some papers on his desk then looked up at Daniel again. "We have run numerous tests, including a brain scan, and I am sorry to say he has already reached advanced stages of dementia, also known as middle dementia. He is in severe cognitive decline. He could remain at this stage for a long time – or not for long. Every patient is different. Some stay at this stage for many years."

Daniel had been prepared for bad news but was shocked at the diagnosis.

"What does this mean exactly?" he asked.

"This means Jack is going to need round-the-clock care. He is at the stage when he would not be able to react in an emergency. He may forget the number for the emergency services, for example. He may not recognise smoke as a danger sign or understand why a smoke detector sounded. He is classed as being extremely vulnerable. People with dementia do not understand time. Three minutes to a dementia sufferer can seem like an hour. For example, if you were going out and you said to him you would only be an hour, the likelihood would be he would start to become anxious. He would not know how long you had been gone and would perhaps go looking for you, putting himself in a very dangerous position. He will most likely have problems with simple technology: using the remote control, the telephone or the stove. He will need constant reminding of how things work. He is likely to start having trouble taking care of himself, shaving, washing properly and even dressing. People with dementia can usually still dress themselves but they are likely to wear the same clothes day after day. They may have difficulty putting their clothes on in sequence; for example, wearing their underwear over their trousers or putting clothes on inside out. Not dressing according to the climate, either wearing too many clothes or not enough." Dr Romano paused.

"Yes, I have noticed Jack struggling with dressing already. It's in my notes," said Daniel sadly.

“Personal care is another issue,” continued the doctor. “A person with dementia does not like being bossed around and may refuse a bath or shower, saying they already washed. The more you try to reason with them, the more they will resist. It can be very trying, frustrating and exhausting. There will be changes in mood, personality and behaviours. No longer having control over their day because of confusion can create a void of hopelessness, depression and anxiety. They become more and more dependent on the carer to organise their day. Compare it to becoming a parent to a newborn baby, when you are desperate for a minute to yourself, even just to go to the toilet in peace.”

“You paint a terrible picture, Dr Romano,” said Daniel. He swallowed the lump that had been forming in his throat. “What treatments and help are available?”

“Well, there are drugs available. I will certainly prescribe some to help slow down some of the symptoms, to help with memory, confidence and daily living. There are other non-drug treatments that can be enormously helpful, like talking therapies, counselling and psychotherapy. These therapies can help the patient come to terms with the diagnosis. They are usually regular one-to-one or group sessions.

“There is also ‘reminisce’ therapy, or life story work, when the patients talk about their past, using pictures or music. This has proven to improve mood and well-being and focuses on the person rather than the dementia. I know this is a lot to take in. Some of it may go over your head at this stage, Steve, but I need to make you aware of what lies ahead. It's not an easy undertaking, caring for someone with dementia.

"We have a fantastic care home in Palermo which offers all of these therapies, alongside healthy eating, activities and other therapies such as massage, aromatherapy and light box therapy. The best care Italy has to offer. I would suggest it might be the best option for Jack if he has the financial means to cover the care cost. I know it's not an easy decision and there will be guilt involved. You have to consider what is best for Jack. You may think you will be able to cope and you want Jack to be in his own surroundings.

"Really, in all honesty, he won't know and he will feel more secure in an environment where there are routines, safety controls, therapies, specialists and people who are highly trained in this field. As next of kin, you will need power of attorney over all of Jack's medical and financial affairs, be his decision maker. Does he have citizenship here in Italy?"

"Yes, he does have citizenship. What if we get a live-in nurse to help care for Jack?" Daniel asked. He couldn't imagine explaining to Jack that he couldn't stay at home.

"Well, that could work. I would agree with that if he were going home to a family who could all contribute to supporting him. For you alone it would be a tremendous effort. Are you planning on staying here for the long term? If not, it would be unfair on you both in the long run. He would also not benefit from all the care home has to offer: the therapies and intense focus on his personal care. I really would recommend the care home for Jack. If he can afford it, it is the best and safest option."

"Oh, he can afford it," confirmed Daniel. "Money is not the problem. I'm the problem – I don't want to let him go."

Daniel left the doctor feeling heartbroken. He did not realise Jack was so unwell. He knew he didn't want to stay in Italy in the long term. The care home the doctor discussed with him did seem like the best option. He still had not made a decision as he walked into the private room where Jack was waiting for him.

"Hey, how are you?" Daniel asked. Jack was sitting in an armchair, his overnight things in a bag on the bed.

"Gareth, where the hell have you been?" Jack asked. "Your mother will be worried sick about me. Does she even know I'm here? They wouldn't let me use the phone to let her know." He started getting upset then, tearful and frustrated.

"Jack, it's me. Daniel. I'm not Gareth," Daniel told him gently, upset to find Jack in this state. He was beginning to think the doctor was right. Jack needed professional care. The doctor had told him it would be best to take him to the care home rather than home, and get him settled in as quickly as possible. It would only be harder in the long run to confuse him by taking him home, then on to the care home. "Come on Jack, there's a place I want you to see," he said sadly.

The care home was bright and clean, the staff friendly and professional. They were shown around the entire building. The private rooms were brightly decorated, with en suites that had a bath and shower. Each bath was fitted with an easy walk-in panel for patients that required them. It was an unwelcome indication of how bad Jack could get. It upset Daniel to think of it.

But Jack's potential room was definitely comfortable and much nicer than Daniel had imagined it would be. It would give Jack a feeling of independence and was not a bit like the old folks' homes in the UK.

Next, they were shown the treatment and therapy rooms. Daniel thought they resembled the treatment rooms he would expect to see in top hotels, and he was impressed. There was an indoor swimming pool and a gym with bikes, treadmills and mats for floor work, yoga and pilates.

Everyone they met greeted them like old friends; there was a happy atmosphere in the home. Even Jack seemed to like it.

The gardens were beautiful. Several small groups convened at different spots. Some were painting, some were sitting in a circle, talking. Daniel guessed correctly that this was one of the therapy groups. Others walked around admiring the different flowers and plants. It certainly seemed like a well organised, safe place. Daniel was sure Jack would receive the best care here. He could not deny it was a better option than taking him home, where he could come to harm. He wouldn't be able to live with himself if Jack injured himself when he was out, or during the night if Daniel was in a deep sleep and did not hear Jack get up. He had discussed the fees for staying here. They were astronomical but Jack could afford it and he was very glad that they had been so successful with their art fraud adventure.

Jack thought he was there for a short break. The doctor and Daniel had both agreed he would not understand the facts of his illness at this stage and the therapy groups would be able to help him come to terms with it, when the time was right. They would be able to give him the tools to help cope with it. In the end, Daniel was grateful to the doctor. He would never have been able to cope alone with the progression of Jack's condition. It would have been sheer folly to even try, especially since his long-term plans did not include staying in Italy.

∞

At the villa, over the course of the next few days, Daniel put the finishing touches to the girls' bedrooms. He was full of excitement at their impending arrival and it took his mind off worrying about Jack.

Chapter 17

Anna

At the airport, Anna checked the passports and the travel documents again.

"Stop stressing," said Michael, laughing at her. "You must have checked them a million times."

"I know, I'm a nervous traveller," Anna replied, looking worried and fraught. "It's the thought of seeing Daniel again," she admitted. "It's been so long and I really did not think I would see him again, ever."

"I know," said Michael, soothingly. "It'll be fine. I'm sure he'll be delighted to see the girls and will want to spend as much time with them as possible. Maybe leaving us with a little time to ourselves."

"Yeah maybe. I just wish I had booked us into a hotel now. It's going to be awkward living with him in the villa."

"He said there was plenty of space, didn't he? I'm sure he'll give us our privacy and it won't be awkward at all," Michael reasoned.

"Mum, can you come and look at the duty free with me?" Eloise interrupted.

"Sure," said Anna, glad of the distraction. Leah lay along

three seats, playing a game on her mobile phone to kill time.

Once they were out of earshot, Michael moved over to sit with her. "I hope you are going to be on your best behaviour. Don't go running to Daddy about how horrible Mummy's new boyfriend is," he told her.

Ignoring him, Leah pulled herself up and looked around for her mother. He sidled along towards her again, grabbing her hand and squeezing it painfully. "Well?" he said.

"Fine, I'll be on my best behaviour," she answered, pulling her hand free. She rubbed it where there were now painful red marks.

"You better be. I'll be keeping a close eye on you," he said, then suddenly put his arm around her, beaming happily as Anna and Eloise returned. Leah freed herself from him and said she was going for a look around the shops. She walked away angry, tears falling from her eyes.

The plane journey was a smooth one. They slept and ate and before they knew it the plane was landing. When they had retrieved their cases, they headed out to see if Daniel was waiting for them. Anna saw him right away; he was waving wildly. He looked the same only more tanned and healthy; Italy had treated him well, she thought as they made their way towards him.

The girls ran into his open arms. Leah especially hugged him tight and took forever to let him go. "Hey," he said, looking at her. “Don’t worry, we are going to spend every minute together. I’ve missed you so much.”

“Me too, Dad, you don’t know how much,” she said, squeezing him again. Daniel was not expecting such an emotional reunion, especially since the last time he saw the girls they had not shown much interest in him.

“Daniel, you look well,” said Anna as she reached out to hug him. “This is Michael – I told you about him.” Daniel faked a smile and reached out to shake Michael’s hand.

“Pleased to meet you,” he lied smoothly.

“Likewise,” answered Michael, with a smile that did not quite reach his eyes.

“Let’s get you all back to the villa. You must be exhausted,” Daniel said into the awkward atmosphere between the two men. “Wait till you see your rooms,” he told the girls excitedly.

In the car, Anna sat in the passenger seat. Daniel told her he had prepared a double bedroom for her and Michael with an en suite.

“I don’t want a double bedroom, Daniel,” she told him quietly.

Daniel was surprised – he assumed they were sleeping together but he said, “It’s no problem, there are plenty of rooms. Why don’t you choose when you get there?” Though he was taken aback he asked no more questions. He didn't want to upset her before they were even settled in. He was also surprised how happy it made him that Anna wanted separate rooms. Maybe their relationship wasn't as serious as he had thought.

At the villa, the girls were delighted with their rooms and all the gadgets and comforts Daniel had provided them with.

"That's too much," said Anna, in awe of it all. She seemed uncomfortable at the thought of how much money he had spent.

"Not at all," answered Daniel. "I've not seen my girls for so long, I've got a lot of making up to do."

Michael said he was tired and wanted to go for a lie down; did he mean to give Anna a chance to talk alone with Daniel? Daniel stifled his pleasure at the thought of having her to himself and poured Anna a drink. They sat on the balcony, soaking up the last of the sun's rays.

"It's beautiful down here," Anna said, sighing happily.

"Yes, it is. But it's been a good few years now and, to be honest, I'm ready to move on soon," Daniel admitted, suddenly looking sad. "I'd love to come home but it just wouldn't be safe for me."

"Talking of home," said Anna, not quite able to make the transition sound like a natural one, "I was watching *Crimewatch* last week and there was a section on art fraud. Apparently an older man dressed as a priest sold a fake painting. There was a composite sketch of him." She was watching Daniel's reaction carefully. He didn't flinch. "Who is it you are staying down here with?" she asked, trying to sound innocent. She could see Daniel thinking. He swirled his drink around awkwardly, debating whether to tell her the truth.

"Jack. I'm living down here with Jack," he said, defeated.

"Who is Jack?" she asked. He figured he had nothing to lose but to tell her the whole story.

"When we broke up, I almost killed myself, Anna. I hit rock bottom. I came home when you had moved in with Susan, found the house empty and thought I had lost you all for good. I took every painkiller I could find and washed them down with vodka."

Anna was visibly shocked but said nothing. She held her breath, waiting for him to go on.

"Anyway, I was unconscious, I guess, when Reggie brought me back to life. He told me he wanted me to rob an old farmhouse and steal two paintings. I didn't want to do it, but he threatened to go to the military police about the incident in Afghanistan. He had me over a barrel. So I agreed – and I was caught in the act. The house belonged to Jack Blair – turns out Jack was Reggie's Commanding Officer. The one who insisted he be medically discharged because he was suffering from PTSD. He wanted revenge on him, too.

“To cut a long story short, Jack paid him off. Then Jack wanted me to paint copies of famous works to sell on for profit. Again he had me over a barrel and I agreed to do it. We successfully sold some and that’s where I got the money from.” Daniel searched Anna’s face for a reaction. He could see she was visibly shocked by his revelation.

“This is unbelievable,” she managed, trying to take it all in. “I cannot believe you did that. Were you not afraid of getting caught? The repercussions?”

“Not really,” Daniel said. “I had lost you and the girls, my job. I had nothing else to lose. It was actually quite exciting. Jack dressed as a priest and gave a phony story of how he came about the paintings, and before we knew it we were making money.

“When Jack was nearly rumbled, he lost his confidence and decided to come down here. I sold a few myself, until one day I had the misfortune to see Reggie in London. He threatened to blow the whistle and that’s when… Well.” He did not finish the sentence.

“When you killed him,” Anna whispered softly.

“Yes,” he confirmed, looking down.

“And Jack – where is he now?” she asked.

“Jack is unwell. He has dementia. It’s so bad I’ve had to put him in a care home,” and Daniel’s eyes filled with unexpected tears.

"Oh, Daniel," Anna put her hand over his. "That must have been a tough decision."

"You've no idea," he said, grateful to have someone to talk it over with. "We had become really good friends. He was more like a father to me than my own. It broke my heart making that decision. I had to admit I couldn't do it alone, look after him. I don't plan to stay here much longer, so I had to make sure he was in a safe place, being well looked after, and he is. He's getting the best care. Thankfully he can afford it. This *Crimewatch* thing… that is Jack but that's the least of his worries now. Even if they catch up with him, which I doubt they will, he wouldn't be fit for prosecution."

Eloise burst through the door. "What are we doing for dinner? I'm starving!" she announced.

"Whatever you want, princess," said Daniel, laughing. "I've got everything in you could possibly wish for, unless you want to go out for tea?"

"I think we're all bushed after the travelling," Anna said, getting up. "Pizza and an early night sound fabulous."

"Yes please," Eloise voiced her approval. "What are we doing tomorrow, Dad?"

"How do you fancy a sail on the *Lucky Lady*?" Daniel asked, laying his hand gently on his daughter's head.

Chapter 18

Michael

Michael chose a room with no others adjoining. He needed his privacy. He called his father to let him know they had arrived.

"What's the plan?" he asked, making himself comfortable on the single bed, and kicking his shoes off onto the floor.

"Can you come to my hotel tomorrow to discuss?" Tommy asked. He was obviously keen to get things underway.

"Sure. I think I can break free. What time?"

"As early as you can," answered Tommy abruptly before hanging up. Michael shut his eyes, wondering what his father had in mind. Whatever it was he would have to go along with it. He was trying to prove to him that he was ready for more responsibility in the family business, that one day he could take over. He let himself fantasise about how things would be. He'd have a tailor make his clothes. He liked clothes and he liked to look smart. He'd drive the best car they owned, or maybe have a chauffeur drive him. All the ladies would be rallying round him. He fell asleep with his thoughts, dreaming dreams of better things ahead.

When he woke up he could smell pizza. He realised he was starving. Wandering down to the kitchen he joined the others for dinner. They were talking about a boat trip in the morning. He had to get out of going. Luckily, Leah made it easy for him as she was insisting Anna join them.

"Would you come too, Michael?" Anna asked, chewing on a pizza crust.

"Actually, do you mind if I don't?" he asked, still trying to think of a reason. "I was thinking of having a chilled day. Maybe go for a jog, read, laze by the pool. Don't you fancy doing that?" he asked her, knowing how much it would annoy Leah.

"Mum, please, you said you would come, too," Leah said, rising to the bait. Anna looked awkwardly at Michael.

"Sorry but I did say I'd go. I thought you'd come, too," she said, looking crestfallen.

"You go, babe," he said. "Have fun, it'll be fine. I'll see you when you get back."

"Okay. If you're sure you don't mind?" Anna still looked uncertain.

When Anna's back was turned Leah gave him a smug look. He stared back at her, his eyes stony. She quickly turned her attention elsewhere. She was still terrified of him but felt marginally safer now that she was with her dad. Daniel was busy clearing up in the kitchen, probably just pretending he hadn't heard their conversation. Michael knew Anna's ex would be secretly delighted he wasn't joining them.

∞

The next morning was mayhem. The girls excitedly got

their stuff together for the sail, shrieking with laughter over breakfast – then they, Daniel and Anna left. Michael stayed in his room until the house fell silent and he knew they were gone.

In the kitchen, he found that Anna had left him a note and breakfast. He tossed the unread note in the bin and scoffed the breakfast. He took the short walk to his father's hotel and when he arrived was surprised to see his sister still there.

"Eve!" he said. "How have you been getting on, making friends with the infamous Daniel?" He grabbed a bottle of water out the fridge and laid across the leather couch.

"He's actually very nice," she answered, protectively.

"Oh dear. Someone's got too close." He shook his head as his father appeared from the adjoining room.

"Yes, indeed," said Tommy, not looking pleased. "I want you to go home now, Eve. I've booked you a late morning flight. Michael will accompany you to the airport to make sure you don't miss it."

Eve looked frustrated but Michael knew by his father's tone that there would be no arguing with him.

"Go and pack," Tommy instructed. "Michael and I have got things to discuss."

Michael watched as Eve leaned over the couch to pick up her shoes. She slammed the door as she left the room.

"Now then, this is what I have in mind," Tommy began in

a low voice. His thin face was taut and his eyes icy cold. "I'm going to arrange a night at the villa, to thank Daniel – or Steve, as he likes to be called – for looking after Eve. You suggest a dinner of some kind. I'm going to bring a bottle, some sweet dessert liqueur laced with valium. When everyone is out for the count, you are going to shoot Daniel through the head on his right side. Then wipe the gun and plant it in his right hand. When you're doing all this, I will be setting a fire that'll rip through the house once we leave. It will look like a murder suicide. We will stay on for a few days, going on excursions and shopping, then we leave Friday. Mission accomplished." Tommy sat back, looking pleased. "Any questions?"

"The kids as well?" asked Michael, trying not to sound bothered.

"Of course, no loose ends," said Tommy, shaking a cigarette from its packet. Michael took one, too, trying not to shake as Tommy lit it with a Zippo. He did not expect that. He knew Daniel was in for it but Anna and the kids… he wasn't expecting that at all.

"Now, I want you to take Eve to the airport and don't let her out of your sight, even for a minute. I don't want her trying to contact Daniel to tip him off. Make sure she boards that flight and watch it take off," Tommy warned. "Eve!" he shouted. "Get your backside in gear, you're going to miss your flight."

Eve came into the room dragging her case behind her, looking stunning in a cream cashmere jumper suit. She bent down behind the couch to buckle her shoes.

"Thank you for all your help sweetheart," said Tommy, hugging her tightly. "You go home and get on with your studies. We'll be back by the weekend."

"Thanks, Dad," she said. Then she stepped back and looked at the floor. "You know that Daniel is full of remorse for Reggie..."

"Uh," Tommy held up a hand. "Just forget about him now." Eve sighed and nodded.

In the car on the way to the airport Michael could feel her looking at him. He gazed at the back of the taxi driver's head.

Then she said, "You can't let him do anything too bad."

He turned his head to look out the window, away from her. "Since when could anyone make Dad do anything?" he asked.

"Michael, listen, this is important. Daniel – he regrets what happened to Reggie, but Reggie was a bad man. He attacked Daniel's wife for heavens' sake. What would you have done?"

Michael continued to stare out the window but he thought about what Eve had said. If someone attacked his wife – if he were married – he would kill that person. No doubt about it.

But this was their uncle. Their flesh and blood. And family was everything. If they did not avenge Reggie's death it would leave them open to anyone who wanted to do them harm. They would be seen as a pushover, a family not worth their salt. Reggie's death had to be avenged, that he was sure about. He just wasn't so sure about Anna and the girls.

As they neared the airport Eve gave it one last shot. "Please Michael, if you can stop him, do it. Do you want to ruin your life? You might end up in prison. Think about yourself, your own future."

Michael could feel her gaze but he refused to turn and look at her. The airport came into view but Eve said nothing more.

"Right, come on, let's get you home," he said as the car pulled up in the drop-off area. Eve climbed out and took her suitcase from the taxi driver, saying nothing more – but Michael noted the determined line of her mouth and hard look in her eyes.

Chapter 19

The Lucky Lady

Daniel handled the *Lucky Lady* with the skill of a seasoned sailor, Anna noticed in awe. It was a beautiful morning and the sunrays bounced off the sea, leaving a diamond effect on the ripples of the gentle waves. The gulls squawked loudly when Eloise threw crusty bread over the side of the boat and the little girl laughed with glee as they swooped in for their takings.

Daniel was planning to sail round to a pretty bay nearby, where they could jump off the boat and swim, then have a leisurely lunch before returning to the villa. Leah lay on a towel on the deck, feeling happy and safe. She looked at her parents chatting together and wished they could keep sailing, away from Michael. She hated him. She wished the rest of her family could see what he was really like, but her mother was blind to it.

"This is so lovely," said Anna, inhaling the fresh sea air deep into her lungs. She looked out at the miles and miles of sea surrounding them.

"How serious is this thing between you and Michael?" Daniel found himself asking, before he had even really thought about it.

"I'm not sure," answered Anna. "I do really like him but Leah… Well, she doesn't seem to like him and that's got my guard up. I can't be with someone who my children don't like, so

I'm kind of hoping this trip will bring them closer. If not, I'm not sure what the future will hold for us."

"That's not like Leah," said Daniel, turning to look at her. "Why does she not like him? Has something happened?"

"No, not at all, I think it might just be teenage angst. She started asking to see you not long after I introduced him. I wonder if she just doesn't like the idea of a new father figure."

"It's not that. He's mean to me," said Leah, interrupting their conversation. She had heard it all from her place on the deck.

"How?" asked Daniel, not perturbed by her interruption.

"When we are all together he's all sweetness and light, but when I was alone with him he called me a spoilt bitch and pulled my hair. He threatens me," she said, crying now. "Mum won't believe me. I tried to record him once but he must have known because he was all kind and nice. Then he turned off my phone and said, 'Do you think I'm bloody stupid?'"

"Leah!" Anna snapped. "Don't use that language."

"I don't use that language, he did!" Leah was indignant. "Why won't you believe me?" She glared at them and then hurtled below deck, away from her parents' shocked faces.

Anna was visibly shaken by her daughter's outburst and sat down on a sun lounger.

"She's very convincing," Daniel said, sitting down next to

her. “How long have you known him?”

“Not long, to be honest,” Anna replied awkwardly. Had she been wrong to doubt Leah’s word?

“I think you need to have a chat with him, find out what’s really going on,” said Daniel, concerned. He hadn’t spoken much to Michael, only a few words here and there. He hadn’t been able to gauge the fellow at all but after Leah’s outburst he planned to get to know him a whole lot better. There was no way he was going to let this slide without finding out exactly what was going on.

Chapter 20

Eve

At the airport, Eve told Michael she was going to the ladies to freshen up.

"Better be quick," Michael told her. "Flight boards in five minutes." She rushed through to the ladies and was dismayed to find a queue for the cubicles. She joined the line and shielded her phone to scroll through the recordings.

She felt so smug at the thought that neither Michael nor her dad had realised she'd managed to record their conversation while she was packing. Thank goodness she'd left her shoes behind the sofa – they had no idea she left her phone on the floor to record what they said when she picked up her shoes, and then retrieved it again when she bent down to do her shoes up.

As she scrolled through the list to make sure the conversation had recorded, Michael poked his head round the door. All the ladies in the queue jumped at his presence, some voicing their displeasure.

"Eve, come on, your flight's boarding," he ordered. Eve slipped her phone back into her bag and sighed loudly.

Slipping past everyone in the queue and rejoining her brother, she said, "For goodness' sake Michael, you can't just burst into the ladies like that."

"I think I just did," he said, grinning, and he grabbed her

case and marched her to departures.

Michael stood legs apart and arms crossed, waiting for her to board the plane. When she looked back she could see him standing at the window, watching. She looked away, scowling. Once on the plane, she took a window seat and looked at the terminal again. Still he stood watching. Eve felt like flicking him a v sign, but decided not to lower herself. Instead she took out her phone and tried to find the recording. To her horror, the battery light on her phone was flashing. She was going to have to charge it before she could listen. Frustrated, she kicked the seat in front.

"Oi! Excuse me," said the passenger, turning to glare at her. Eve apologised profusely. She found her charger and prayed her phone would charge quickly, so she could hear what her father had in mind for Daniel. She felt trapped and gravely concerned for him.

Chapter 21

Daniel

Daniel went below deck to see Leah. “Hey you,” he said, nudging her as she lay with her back to him. “What’s going on, honey?” She was sobbing, her pillow wet with tears.

“Mum doesn’t believe me,” she said, turning to face him. Her pretty face was puffy and red, with strands of hair stuck to her cheeks.

“Tell me, then,” Daniel coaxed, gently stroking her hair away from her face.

“He acts one way around her and another way when I’m alone with him,” she said, gulping back sobs. “He’s not a nice person, Dad.” She stared into his eyes, her own childlike with fear. “He frightens me; can I stay here with you?”

“Oh Leah, what would your mum do without you?” Daniel wrapped his arms round her and scooped her into a hug. “Having you stay with me would be a dream come true for me, but it would break your mother’s heart.”

“Why did you guys have to split up?” she asked sadly.

“It’s very complicated,” Daniel told her, trying to avoid being patronising. “I’ll tell you the whole story one day – but not today. Can we try having some fun? Eloise is up there ready for a swim. Are you coming?”

“Yeah,” she said. “Just give me a minute.”

True to her word, Leah joined the three of them on deck a short time later. She seemed to have forgotten about her earlier distress, as she leapt off the boat and went swimming. Daniel had brought snorkelling equipment and the girls followed fish through the tranquil waters. It turned into the perfect day. The family were exhausted as they headed back towards port.

∞

When they arrived at the villa, the telephone was ringing.

"Hello?" Daniel answered, thinking it might be the care home about Jack.

"Steve, it's Tommy. How are you?" said the voice at the other end.

"Tommy! I'm great thanks, how are you? How is Eve? I've not managed to see her recently."

"Eve's gone home. She had to get back to her studying," Tommy told him, and Daniel's heart sank. He was sad to hear she had left without saying goodbye. He regretted telling her everything now. She probably hated him and he could hardly blame her.

"Oh. I'm sorry to hear that. I would've liked to say goodbye," he answered.

"I'll pass on your regards," Tommy replied. "And I wondered if I might come by some evening to drop in some wine and thank you for taking care of her while I was away."

"There's no need. It was my pleasure," answered Daniel, still smarting at Eve's sudden departure.

"No, I insist," said Tommy. "Would tonight be a good time?"

"Sure," answered Daniel, absently. "We'll be here."

∞

Anna and the girls had gone for a short nap when they got back from the boat trip. Daniel was lying on a lounger by the pool when Michael came back.

"Hi, is Anna around?" he asked Daniel.

"She's having a sleep, tired out, not used to the sea air," answered Daniel, giving a half smile. "Why don't you join me? It'd be good to have a chat."

"Great," answered Michael. He sat down but Daniel could see he wasn't keen on the idea.

"So, how did you meet Anna?" he asked, shading his eyes from the sun's glare.

"I went for a haircut, she cut it," answered Michael, a little abruptly.

"Aren't you a little young for her?" Daniel dared to ask.

"Not really. It's not a problem," answered Michael, lying back on the lounger and turning his gaze away from Daniel's penetrating stare.

"And the girls? How do you find dating someone with

children?" Daniel persisted.

"It's not a problem. As a teaching assistant, I'm used to kids," he explained, sounding just slightly defensive.

Daniel thought he would dig deeper. "Teenage girls, though, they can be a handful. Take Leah, for instance. How have you been getting on with her?" asked Daniel, watching Michael carefully.

"Leah's fine. Sure she gives me a hard time sometimes. I think it's difficult for her seeing her mum give her time to someone other than her and Eloise," he explained.

"She told me she's frightened of you." Daniel thought he'd get straight to the point. "Why would she be frightened of you?"

Michael sat in silence for a few moments, then turned to face Daniel. He was a handsome man, with dark hair and the greenest eyes he'd ever seen. For a moment, Daniel thought he looked somehow familiar and then he was struck by who the resemblance was with. Reggie. Michael reminded him of Reggie. The same dark hair, the same shape of face.

"Do you wear contact lenses?" Daniel asked.

"No," Michael looked confused. "Why do you ask?"

"You remind me of someone I used to know. You'd be the spit of him if your eyes were brown." Daniel eyed Michael suspiciously.

Michael stood up abruptly. "I'm going to find Anna," he

said. Daniel watched him stride away. He had the same build as Reggie, too. It was an unnerving coincidence.

∞

When Anna and the girls finally woke, Daniel told them he was expecting a visitor. He told them about Tommy and his daughter Eve, whom he had been keeping an eye on whilst Tommy was away.

"Was she hard to watch?" asked Anna, turning away as soon as she said it.

"No, not at all," answered Daniel, picking up what he considered a jealous tone. "Eve's a lovely young woman; and when I say young, I mean too young for me." Anna blushed.

"I took her out on the boat and to the gallery in Palermo, otherwise she would have been on her own," Daniel explained. "Tommy just wants to come round to thank me; though he really doesn't have to."

"We should make a nice dinner," Michael suggested. "Since everyone is tired after the boat trip today, I don't mind helping."

"That's kind of you," Anna said, rubbing his back gently. "I'll help, too. Daniel, why don't Michael and I prepare dinner and you can chill out for a bit?"

"Well, if you're sure. There's plenty of food in," Daniel said, looking forward to spending time with his daughters. "Hey girls, do you fancy a walk down to the harbour? I'll buy you an ice cream." The girls happily agreed, and they left Anna and Michael to prepare the meal.

∞

They arrived back to delicious aromas coming from the kitchen. "That smells wonderful," said Daniel. "What have you made?"

"We've made a prawn cocktail for starters, then a seafood linguine, followed by a lemon cheesecake for dessert," Anna told him.

"You're making my mouth water. I'll just go and change into a fresh shirt." Leaving the kitchen, Daniel suddenly stopped and turned back. "Oh, and before I forget, don't be surprised if Tommy calls me Steve. I think I remind him of someone back home." Daniel turned away again and made his way to his bedroom.

"Can you girls go and smarten up a bit, too," Anna instructed.

"What's wrong with the way we are?" grumbled Leah, looking down at her shorts and t-shirt.

"Nothing but I'd rather you put on a nice dress, since someone's coming for dinner." The girls reluctantly went to get changed, and Anna headed off to have a shower and freshen up, too. When they all assembled in the living room shortly afterwards, everyone looked smarter and ready to greet their guest.

At 8pm, the doorbell rang. Daniel let Tommy in, shaking his hand, then took him through to introduce him to the family. After an aperitif, they all sat down at the table for the meal.

"This food is delicious," Tommy said, raising a fork of seafood linguini.

"Thank you," answered Michael, raising his glass in a cheers motion. "I made it myself."

"Sorry, what did you say you do again? Are you a chef?" asked Tommy with a half-smile.

"No, I work with children," Michael answered, stroking Leah's hair. She had been seated next to Michael by her mum, and though she was obviously reluctant, said nothing. But at Michael's touch, she shook her head away. The move did not go unnoticed by Daniel, who was sitting opposite.

"Leah, why don't you sit beside your old dad?" he suggested. Without hesitation, she passed her plate across the table, then lifted her chair and carried it round to her father's side. She gave Michael a smug look as she sat down.

Daniel, too, looked at Michael, then glanced at Tommy. He frowned and looked back at Michael. They had the same jawline, the same chiselled features, the same mannerisms... Daniel felt suddenly uneasy. Perhaps he would need to keep his wits about him tonight.

After the main course, Tommy produced a bottle and presented it to Daniel. "To say a huge thank you for looking after my daughter, I bought you this beautiful liqueur. I thought we might share it while eating our dessert," he announced. "It is low in alcohol and very sweet so the children can enjoy a drop, too."

"Oh, I don't think that's a good idea," protested Anna immediately.

"Mum," scolded Leah, "it's only a drop."

"Yes, a drop will be okay," Michael chimed in. Leah looked at him suspiciously. She didn't trust him and wasn't sure why he was backing her up.

"Okay, fine," Anna relented. "Only the smallest drop." She left the table to find some shot glasses.

When the doorbell rang, Michael jumped and Tommy looked annoyed. Daniel rose to answer the door. He was first shocked and then very happy to find Eve at the doorstep.

"Eve!" He exclaimed. "What are you doing here? I thought you went home?"

He was joined at the door by Tommy, who almost pushed him aside. "What are you doing?" he asked angrily. His face was almost red with rage.

"It was rude of me to leave without thanking Steve and saying goodbye. I made the rash decision to get the flight straight back," Eve explained, looking at Daniel and ignoring her dad's angry expression.

"That was a crazy thing to do," admonished Tommy. "Bloody stupid in fact. I told you to go home."

"Well, I'm here now," said Eve, making her way into the dining area, where the girls and Michael still sat, and Anna stood watching. Michael gave her a stony look and shook his head.

"Hi," said Anna pleasantly. "I'm Anna. Sit down, I'll bring you some food." She fussed around the new guest. Eve sat down, still refusing to look at her father.

"I was just going to pour everyone some liqueur," said Tommy, looking at her pointedly. "Won't you have some?"

"No, thank you," said Eve, finally looking directly at her dad. "I'll wait until after dessert."

"If you say so," he shrugged. "Would you excuse me while I go for a smoke in the garden?" Without waiting for a reply, Tommy left the room, indicating to Michael to go with him.

As soon as they were out of view, Eve grabbed the bottle and poured two shot glasses for her dad and brother.

"Don't – touch – these," she warned the others, quietly and firmly. She fled into the kitchen and quickly found a similar looking drink, which she poured into all the other glasses. She placed a glass at each chair, making sure the two drinks from her father's bottle were out of reach of everyone else. "Remember –

don't touch them," she repeated.

"What's going on, Eve?" Daniel asked her urgently.

"I'll explain later, I promise," she pleaded.

Too puzzled to chat, the group were silent when Tommy and Michael returned to the table.

"Let's say a toast to a wonderful meal," said Eve, smiling widely. Tommy noted the full liqueur glasses and assumed Eve had eaten dessert. He was happy to see she had poured one for herself; it might be helpful if she was conked out for a while.

"Dad," Eve said suddenly, as Leah picked up her glass. "Why don't you drink yours first? Prove it's not too strong for the girls." Tommy glared at her while everyone waited for him to drink his shot.

"It's fine," said Michael impatiently, picking up his shot glass and downing it in one. It suddenly struck him that this was the perfect way to get out of his father's murderous plan. He had no qualms about getting rid of Daniel but the idea of hurting Anna and the kids did not sit well with him at all. "See, I'm not drunk."

Tommy stared at Michael, then felt everyone's gaze on him. He picked up his glass and downed it in one. "Now everyone else," he said quickly. Perhaps he would be strong enough to overcome the sleep he knew this drink would cause; he had to risk it. Damn Eve. He could happily throttle her right now.

And then, to his relief, everyone downed their drinks. He

watched them carefully, waiting for a reaction; then he quickly excused himself, went to the bathroom and stuck his fingers down his throat. Before he could even gag, he crumpled to the floor and fell asleep.

∞

When Tommy woke up, Eve was standing over him with a look of triumph on her face.

"What did you do, Eve?" he croaked, trying and failing to sit up.

"It's over, Dad," she said evenly. "Daniel and his family have gone. It's time we all went home and got on with our lives."

"Where did they go?" he asked, shaking the heaviness from his head.

"They escaped on the *Lucky Lady* and should be miles away by now," she said, looking smug.

"Oh, I doubt that very much," Tommy laid back down and closed his eyes. "We put a bomb on the *Lucky Lady*, in case they did try to escape. It's probably gone off by now."

Eve turned and ran out the villa and into the night, down to the dock where the *Lucky Lady* had been anchored. It was missing from its berth. She peered into the darkness across the ocean but could see nothing. The sudden explosion was no more than a muffled bang but the orange blaze that flashed into the black sky then settled into a shimmering fire in the distance had Eve sinking to her knees. She sobbed tears of frustration and rage.

Tommy, breathless, sank down beside her. “Come on, our work here is done,” he said quietly. “ Let’s go home.”

Chapter 22

The Fraud Squad

The *Crimewatch* programme had been given the same name time and time again. Jack Blair. A caller, who did not want to be identified, claimed Jack Blair was living in Mondello Beach with a person named Steve Arnold. The caller had told officers this was a fake name and his true identity was Daniel Edgar. He claimed Daniel had murdered Reggie Raymond Brown and should be brought to justice for it. Hanging up the receiver, Rob Imrie felt that he had done his bit and hoped justice would be served, by Tommy or the law.

Jack Blair was deemed unfit to stand trial due to his escalating dementia. A warrant for Daniel Edgar's arrest was issued. He was nowhere to be found in Palermo or Mondello Beach.

The fraud squad closed the case on the fake paintings.

The murder case into Reggie Raymond Brown reopened.

Part 4

Chapter 1

Eve

At home in England, Eve cut off all ties from her father. He was dead to her. He was a murderer who had taken the lives of Daniel, Anna and their daughters. She felt sick to her stomach every time she thought of that night. Eve had been so certain she was in time to rescue them all. That Tommy had outwitted her and killed the family was devastating.

The remains of the boat were retrieved. No bodies recovered. It was assumed they had been blown to pieces or simply lost at sea. Eve was heartbroken and vowed never to forgive Tommy.

Authorities in Italy put the explosion down to a problem on the boat. But Eve knew it would not have served her well to go to the police and tell them about the bomb. She knew she would be implicated. With a heavy heart, she returned home and threw herself into her studies.

∞

After five years of hard slog, Eve could sit in the lounge of her stylish Hampstead Heath townhouse and gaze at the spoils of her success.

An esteemed fashion designer, she lived a glamorous lifestyle, travelling extensively to fashion shows in New York, Paris, Milan and Madrid. At twenty-six she was living the dream.

Her forward-thinking fashion produced styles to suit ladies and girls of all ages. Her designs ranged from affordable to high end. Eve Brown was a household name and her fashion brand 'Achieve' was recognisable in every shop. She was proud of herself. She had worked her fingers to the bone, sometimes staying up all night to produce items that would stand out from the rest. And it had all been worth it.

Eve had not spoken to her brother Michael since their return but lately he had been trying to contact her. So far she had ignored his calls. He left endless messages telling her he had wanted no part in their father's plan, hence having so willingly drank the laced liqueur he knew would send him to sleep. He did not want any part in killing Anna and the girls. Eve noticed he said nothing about Daniel.

Michael claimed he had no knowledge of Tommy planting the bomb. Eventually he wore Eve down and she agreed to see him.

Slowly but surely, they rebuilt their broken relationship and she found she was happy to have her brother back in her life – although she would always be wary of him.

Chapter 2

Michael

Michael had been a nervous wreck that night at the villa. He had no qualms about getting rid of Daniel but the thought of harming Anna and the girls had not sat well with him. He did not agree with his father that they should be killed as well. After all, what had Anna done? She was not involved in Reggie's death.

When Eve had returned and he realised he was going to have to drink the laced liqueuer, he saw it as a welcome get out, glad that he would fall into oblivion. Had he known about the bomb, maybe he would have done something. But it was too late now. What was done was done.

When they returned home, Tommy was furious with him. Michael had managed to wriggle his way out of the situation. He told his father he had downed the drink thinking it would mean his father would not have to. But Tommy's expression was doubtful and he told Michael he would have to work hard to earn his trust in future.

Michael worked closely with Tommy, learning more about the business. The cars they bought and sold, the people they dealt with, the lucrative, not so legal, business on the side, including the smuggling of stolen goods. Tommy told him sternly that they never got involved in actually stealing goods but could easily pass them on without the fear of getting caught.

Tommy ensured they dealt with the same people he had dealt with for years. No new faces. Michael was keen to impress his dad, kept his head down and worked hard. He enjoyed wearing smart suits and he felt important as he shadowed his father and accompanied him to meetings.

Eventually, Michael was given a team of his own to use as he wanted. This was his chance to shine and show his father he was worth his salt. The family business was growing and Michael planned to run the whole thing himself one day. It cramped his style to have his father on his back all the time, sometimes putting him down in front of the men. Michael had to suck it up right now but his day would come. He was sure of it.

Tommy had been crankier than ever since returning from Italy. He was upset that Eve had cut him off. He missed his daughter. He was aware of her growing success and was bursting with pride. It killed him that he could not show her just how proud he was of her. He tried time and again to connect with her but she rejected all his efforts, much to his dismay. He decided to enlist Michael to help him rekindle his relationship with her.

It took Michael a long time to persuade Eve to see him, and a lot of begging, something he loathed doing, but if it got him in his dad's good books, he was willing to do it. Eventually, he wore Eve down and they were rebuilding their relationship. In truth, he was not that bothered about seeing Eve again – it meant more to Tommy than to him. All he had to do was gain her trust and then suggest that she let their father back into her life. It would take time and patience. Michael was certain he could pull it off. His place in the business depended on it.

Chapter 3

Tommy

Tommy had been livid when Eve returned to Mondello unannounced. She had done her best to foil his plans but she had underestimated her father's determination. The secret to Tommy's success was always to have a 'plan b'. He could never have imagined Eve returning to try to rescue Daniel and his family but he had thought it a possibility they would discover Tommy's true intentions and avoid the laced drink altogether. He had taken the extra measure of planting the bomb on the *Lucky Lady*. It was the obvious means of escape.

Tommy's anger at his daughter evaporated when his foresight saw the family killed, and cleaner than he had originally planned. There was no suspicion. The authorities put the explosion down to a fault with the boat's engine. Tommy and his family had been free to return home and carry on with their lives. Tommy's father was pleased to hear that Reggie's death had been avenged. He did not need to hear the details; for him that was enough.

The only fly in the ointment now was Eve. Tommy needed her in his life. She was his child, his pride and joy and he would do anything to get her back. Right now, he was depending on Michael to make sure it happened.

He was secretly pleased with Michael. He had been

showing up early for work, working hard, following direction and taking his put downs. He was leading his new team. He worked well with them, showed good leadership skills and was fair but firm with the men. They seemed to respect him. Tommy was testing him, and so far Michael was passing. But his biggest test he was yet to pass – getting Eve back in Tommy's life. Time would tell if he could accomplish this. Tommy was counting on him.

Chapter 4

Eve

Michael was impressed with Eve's stylish townhouse. It was modern and fresh, and equipped with all the latest designer technology and security. Her living area was minimalist, spacious, with large windows overlooking Teil Green and the beautiful Kidderpore Hall. There was a large, open plan kitchen, complete with all mod cons, and a big, opulent dining table, with chairs the colour of Champagne dotted around it. The table displayed an impressive vase of orange and yellow flowers, and the generous breakfast bar, with seating around it, made it a great space for parties. There was a further reception room on the ground floor with access to a private balcony, and upstairs was a master bedroom with en suite and built-in wardrobes. There were three other bedrooms, all complete with en suites and wardrobes. Just moments away from Hampstead Village, Eve felt as though she lived in rural serenity while having easy access to the city. Michael could see why she loved her home and was impressed that she had managed to accomplish so much in just five years. He was proud of her.

They were having a quiet supper together before she had to leave. The next day she was heading for a fashion show in Madrid, one of her favourite destinations. She had been working tirelessly on her new collection to be displayed in Madrid's fashion week for the first time. It was nice to unwind and chat with Michael before the madness began in the morning. She was booked on an early flight and it would be nonstop hard work until after the fashion show. She planned to stay in Madrid to unwind for a few days, before returning at the weekend.

"I'm so proud of you," said Michael, looking around again at the beauty of her home. "You've really achieved so much. Dad is so proud of you, too."

"Stop," she interrupted, putting up her hand. "I don't want to hear about Dad."

"I know you don't," said Michael warily. "It's just he misses you so much. I've never seen him like this. He's the picture of abstract misery and cantankerous as hell."

"I don't care, Michael, he should have thought of that before he killed an innocent family." Eve was unbreakable in her distaste for their father. "He's a murderer and I don't want to hear any more about him. Do you understand?"

Michael could see there would be no easy way to get Eve to forgive their father. This was going to be a far bigger challenge than he imagined but somehow he had to succeed – his future depended on it.

They finished their supper and changed the subject. Eve said she had to get an early night, so Michael gave her a hug, thanked her for supper and wished her well. They arranged to catch up on her return. As he made his way to his car, Michael thought hard about how he could bring his father and sister back together. It was going to take something extreme, that was for sure. A plan began to formulate in his head. He needed to talk to Tommy.

Chapter 5

Michael & Tommy

At work the next day, Tommy was busy in meetings all morning. Finally, after lunch, Michael managed to pin him down.

"I saw Eve last night," he began, then stopped abruptly. This was always a sore subject to bring up.

"And?" said Tommy impatiently.

"She's still adamant about not seeing you," Michael told him awkwardly.

"Well, that's no big surprise," and Tommy sighed. He was hoping to hear better news. He knew it was not going to be easy to talk Eve round. She could be very stubborn when she wanted to.

"I have a plan, though, that might just work," said Michael, smiling widely. "If she thought you were sick, really sick, I'm sure the ice in her heart would melt. She would want to see her poor ill dad." Tommy walked around the table to pour them more coffee, clearly mulling over what Michael had said.

"You know son, I think you might just have solved the problem." He handed Michael his refill and patted him on the back, proudly. "You're not as daft as you look are you?" he laughed. "When she comes back from Madrid, you can tell her I've been having terrible stomach problems. The doctors are not sure what it is, but it's likely to be something serious. She won't come running at that but if we keep it going you can lead her to believe it's not looking good for me. Maybe it would be my dying wish to see her."

"Consider it done," said Michael, delighted he was back in his father's good books. Now all he had to do was convince Eve. It would take time but he was sure this plan would work and soon the family would be back together.

Chapter 6

Madrid

Eve had the familiar butterflies she always had in the run-up to a huge fashion event. The fashion week in Madrid was no exception. A must-attend event for all designers and models from all over the world, it was the perfect platform to showcase new designs on an international level, and a chance for Eve to shine. She had been working on her new collection for 'Achieve' for months and was more than happy with the collection she was about to show.

For the first time, she was introducing a menswear line, and she was particularly proud of it. With an audience consisting of buyers, Instagram influencers, wholesalers, dealers, marketing professionals and media, it was imperative that the collection was flawless. There was a lot riding on it.

She needn't have worried. When she saw the models strutting down the runway in her clothes, she was overwhelmed by how good they looked. Her hard work had paid off. The menswear collection was 1950s inspired. It consisted of suits, sports coats, slacks and sweaters with a modern twist, the logo 'Achieve' attached somewhere on all items in a small metallic strip. The music chosen for the menswear collection was hits from the 50s, in keeping with the theme, which segued into music from the current decade to illustrate the modernisation of the garments.

The ladies' collection was just as impressive. Eve had chosen to modernise 1960s inspired clothing, which included A-line miniskirts, contrast collar shift dresses, textured tights, low-heel flats, tall boots, swing coats, floppy hats, Audrey Hepburn-inspired Capri pants, sleeveless polo neck tops and, to complete the look, retro sunglasses. The music was from the 60s, then, as in the menswear show, music was added from the current decade.

Back at her hotel, Eve collapsed into bed. She was exhausted but exhilarated. It was a heady feeling. Tonight could not have gone better. She had enjoyed watching the other designers' showcases and she had been interviewed extensively. Her new collection would be rolled out to all the stores she already supplied to, both designer and high street, with some new contracts added into the mix. It was all she could have hoped for and the media coverage would only add to her global success.

Now the show was over, she was happy to have some downtime. She planned to sightsee in Madrid, meander around the markets, sample the local food and drink – be a tourist, visiting the museums, cathedrals and, of course, shopping.

∞

Eve planned on having a long, leisurely lie in, then a massage, swim and sauna. The perfect way to unwind after all the stress preparing for the fashion show. She deserved it. In the afternoon, she left the hotel on foot. Everywhere she wanted to go was in walking distance and she was in no rush. She planned to take her time and make sure everything she did today was at her leisure. Dressed in a cream maxi dress, with training shoes for comfort, Eve looked effortlessly lovely, her dark hair pinned up loosely in a scruffy bun. She wore round sunglasses to protect her eyes from the glaring sun, and she looked stylish and chic.

Her walk led her to the Royal Palace, which she had thought she might visit. However, there was a huge queue to gain entrance. Eve decided to visit the Sabatini Gardens instead. She had a pleasant walk around before finding a bench to rest on. She realised she was hungry and continued her walk, until she reached San Miguel Market. There was an abundance of stalls selling beautifully prepared tapas of all sorts; the smells made her mouth water. The market had super desserts to choose from, and chocolate, wine and sangria. Eve was spoilt for choice. She selected some tapas and a glass of white wine to wash it down, then found a seat where she could lazily people watch while she ate.

Happy and satisfied, Eve watched the crowds meander around the market stalls, chattering and pointing at the goods on offer. As she stood up to leave, a man wearing a stylish linen suit caught her eye. There was something familiar about him, the way he walked, the tilt of his head, the dark hair, his serious expression. It couldn't be… The man she was looking at, fewer than fifty steps away from her, was just like Daniel. She scanned the area to see if he was with anyone. Her eyes nearly popped out of her head when she saw him put his arm around a petite, dark-haired lady.

When the lady turned her face to his and stretched up to kiss him, there was no doubt that it was Anna. Daniel and Anna.

The shock was immediately displaced by joy and Eve sprinted to meet them. She was so happy they were alive and well, tears flooded down her cheeks. By the time she reached them she was in a state of delirium.

"Daniel, is it really you?" she called, breathless. Daniel turned round and the shock on his face almost matched hers.

"Eve," he said simply, releasing Anna and holding out his arms for her to fly into.

"I thought you were dead," she said, sobbing into his linen suit. She detached herself from Daniel and turned to Anna for a hug. Then she stepped back and they stood staring at each other in wonder, laughing and crying simultaneously.

Chapter 7

Daniel

Daniel had been shocked and pleased to see Eve on his doorstep in Palermo, then thoroughly puzzled by her behaviour. When she poured the drinks and told them in no uncertain terms not to touch those for Tommy and Michael, all they could do was trust her.

Tommy and Michael had downed the shots and Michael fell asleep five minutes later. Tommy had gone to the bathroom, where he was found asleep on the bathroom floor. Clearly the drink had been laced with a powerful sedative.

Eve quickly explained that Tommy was Reggie's brother and that he was out for revenge. She revealed that Michael, her brother, was also in on the plan. Anna was horrified. Eve told Daniel that, once she had got to know him, she realised he was not the evil monster her father had painted him to be. She had tried very hard to persuade him to drop his plan. When she finally heard the recorded conversation between her father and brother, and what they had planned for the family, she had returned to Italy to try to stop them. She told them to gather some essentials together and leave – immediately.

Eve drove them to the dock and the *Lucky Lady*. They said their goodbyes and she watched as they sailed away, before returning to the villa to confront her father and brother.

∞

All this Eve knew – the trio made their way to Daniel and Anna's home so they could fill Eve in on what had happened after they had said their goodbyes.

Daniel could not believe Eve was in Madrid. The likelihood of her spotting him in such a populated place was mind-blowing.

"What are you doing here?" he asked, as he drove them to his house.

"I've just done a fashion show," she told him. "It was exhausting so I decided to treat myself to a few days off and explore Madrid. More importantly, what are you doing here, Daniel? I really thought you were all dead."

"Let's get back to the house first, I'll tell you all about it. We're nearly there." Daniel wanted to concentrate on his driving, still not used to the busy Spanish roads.

Daniel and Anna had rented a townhouse in a gated complex. Access to the property was through a beautiful garden, which surrounded the entire house and had an attractive Andalusian-style patio at the back. The home had a stately entrance with a classic, armoured door. Inside, there was a luxurious hall with a wide staircase to the upstairs bedrooms.

"This place is amazing," said Eve, as she entered the hallway and looked around.

"We're only renting," Daniel told her. "Still not sure where we will end up. Blending in here right now."

"Come through to the kitchen," suggested Anna. "I'll make us some coffee." The kitchen was bright and airy, and looked out on the beautiful back garden. They decided to take their coffee outside.

"So, what happened?" asked Eve. She was desperate to know how the family had survived.

Daniel took a deep breath, and then explained. "When we got on the *Lucky Lady*, we had not sailed far when I realised there was a strong smell of cigarette smoke on board. I found some butts and, although I wasn't one hundred percent sure it was Tommy's brand, I had the feeling he had been there. Obviously, we were all on edge after what had just happened, we were in shock and a heightened sense of apprehension. I wondered what he would have been doing on the boat. My intuition was telling me we had to get off, and get off quickly. We jumped into the sea and swam back to shore. It was terrifying in the dark but we had no choice.

"When we heard the explosion and saw the flames, we knew we had just cheated death. When we got back to shore we took shelter on a boat belonging to a friend of Jack's. He was back home in the UK and I knew where he kept the key. His family had left clothes onboard, so we all found something to wear, though nothing really fit! We slept for a couple of hours then I went back to the villa to get our passports and money. We caught a bus to Catania airport – the next flight was to Madrid so we took it, still in these ridiculously ill-fitting clothes. We must have looked a right sight. No one cared. We had survived." Daniel suddenly choked and looked down at the ground.

"I can't believe this," said Eve, placing her coffee cup on the table and leaning forward. "All this time I thought you were dead. I've not spoken to my father since. I tried so hard to talk him out of his revenge plan but it was impossible. When he put me on the plane I listened to the conversation he had with my brother – I had recorded it on my phone. I knew I had to return and try to stop him."

"Without you we would all have died, Eve, there is no doubt about that," said Daniel, reaching out to touch her arm. "You have always been in our thoughts. I wanted to reach out to somehow let you know that we had survived but it was too dangerous."

"We'll always be grateful to you, Eve," Anna added, tears making her eyes glisten. "I was shocked that Michael was involved. Later, when Daniel and I discussed it, Daniel told me Michael looked like Reggie. If he'd had brown eyes he would have been the double of him. We had not thought it was possible they were related but it all began to make sense."

Eve nodded. “They are very similar. Only their eyes are a different colour.”

“It’s all so unbelievable,” said Anna, shaking her head. She was distraught at the thought she had put her daughters in danger through her relationship with Michael.

“Well, the one good thing that came out of it all is that I have my family back,” said Daniel, looking lovingly at Anna. “I never thought it would happen. I could never have imagined it happening this way, that’s for sure!”

With the news of how Daniel and Anna had survived, they and Eve settled back into a more relaxed conversation. Eve told them of her success as a fashion designer. She learned that Daniel was teaching art at a local school. Anna was working as a hairdresser in a salon not far from where they lived. Eloise was enrolled at school, whilst Leah was studying at college.

When the girls came home, they were delighted to see Eve, and even more delighted by the fact she was a designer. They told her they had some of her clothing range and ran to show her the items, with the brand tag ‘Achieve’ on them. They were starstruck and told her how much they loved her style.

Eve agreed to stay for supper with the family, before returning to her hotel. She felt like she was dreaming. She was so happy to have found them and to know they were all alive and well. They enjoyed a delicious supper, with sangria and a calorific chocolate dessert.

Happy and relaxed, Eve thought nothing of Eloise picking up her phone to take pictures of Eve sitting between her parents.

Daniel finally drove Eve back to her hotel. Though Anna had suggested she stay with them, Eve was happy to go back to the hotel, where all her things were. She had plans for the next day or two.

They arranged to meet at the Royal Palace in a few days so they could spend more time together before saying their goodbyes.

Chapter 8

Eve

After returning to her hotel room, Eve took a long bath. She was exhausted. She thought about all the tears she had shed for Daniel and his family, the heartbreak their deaths had caused her. She wondered if she would have been so successful with her fashion brand, if this had not happened.

She had thrown herself into her work to try to erase the memories of what had happened. To stop the depression that had followed. What a strange coincidence seeing them today. If she had looked another way, sat longer in the gardens, she would have missed them altogether, would still be unaware of their survival.

She was so thankful and happy. She went to bed and slept soundly until mid-morning the following day. She was going to spend the day shopping and had arranged to meet Daniel and his family on her last day, before she returned home.

∞

Eve bought bags of beautiful clothes and jewellery to take home. She always liked to buy souvenirs of the places she visited. She had dinner in the hotel restaurant and went to bed early, tired and happy. She was looking forward to seeing Daniel and his family the next day. She was interested to hear his plans. She knew he wanted to go back to the UK one day and wondered if it was on the cards for them.

∞

The next day, Daniel, Anna and the girls were waiting for her at the Royal Palace. They waved the tickets they had bought, and Eve was relieved they would not have to join the queue that had already started to build.

The group walked through the palace – the official residence of the Spanish royal family – with their eyes shining. Lavish halls, banqueting rooms, the throne room, residential areas, the Royal Armoury, the Royal Pharmacy... Leah and Eloise pointed and gasped.

Daniel was particularly keen on seeing the art exhibition.

"So, what are your plans for the future?" Eve asked him as they meandered around the palace, arm in arm. Anna was being rushed excitedly by the girls from one exhibit to another.

"You know, I would love nothing more than to return home to Yorkshire. But I have to make sure it is safe for us to do so," Daniel told her. "Also, I want to return to Palermo to see Jack. He has been on my mind the whole time. I wonder if he even realises I'm no longer there. What about you Eve? Have you met anyone yet? I can't believe you are still single."

"I've been so busy for the last five years, I've honestly not had time for relationships. But yes, it would be nice to meet someone," she told him, squeezing his arm.

"I've no doubt in my mind that you will," said Daniel,

smiling. "And a lucky guy he will be." The rest of the day passed by so pleasantly, Eve relaxed and happy for the first time in such a long time. But all too soon it was time for them to say their goodbyes.

Eve promised to visit them again someday and said she would keep in touch via WhatsApp. Only Eve had other social media accounts – the girls were well aware of the importance of keeping their father's identity as Daniel Edgar unknown. He still used the fake name Steve Arnold. Daniel wasn't sure if he was still under investigation for Reggie's murder, and Jack's appearance on *Crimewatch* had made him realise he could take no chances.

Chapter 9

Michael

Michael squinted through the windscreen and blustery rain as he drove to Eve's house. She would think he was there to hear about how she'd got on with her fashion show but his plan was to begin to spin the tale of their father's pretend illness.

Michael was a good liar. He had no qualms about deceiving his sister, if it got him in his father's good books. He was doing well working for his father, he had a great team and they respected him. Michael was tough on them when he needed to be and generous when he felt they deserved it. He was looking for a way to really impress Tommy and had been chatting with some new faces he had been introduced to by one of his team. They had some interesting things to say about a haul of stolen jewellery they needed to smuggle out of the country. They thought Michael was just the man to help them. Michael knew Tommy was wary of new faces, though. He wasn't sure whether he should tell his father about it or to go it alone. He could tell him of his success once he made his money. It could be the opening he was looking for, to excel in his father's eyes.

He put on a huge smile as Eve opened the door to him. She looked happy and refreshed, and told him all about her success at the show. There was something else, though, he thought; she looked like a weight had been lifted. She looked younger, stress free.

Since they had returned from Italy, she had gone into a severe depression. She had thrown herself into her studies and had achieved so much in a relatively short period of time, she always had a demeanour of sadness. Now, though, Michael thought there was a change in his sister and he wondered why.

"Did you meet anyone in Madrid?" he asked, thinking perhaps she had met a new man. She had not been involved with anyone that he knew of for years. He thought it a waste; Eve was a stunning girl. Eve jumped at the question and Michael thought he detected a look of guilt.

"No," she answered – too quickly.

"Right," he said, unconvinced. She was definitely hiding something.

When she went to the bathroom, he picked up her phone and began scrolling through the photos, expecting to find evidence of a new boyfriend on the scene.

When he arrived at the photo of Eve sitting between Daniel and Anna, he paled. It was like looking at ghosts. He threw the phone back down where Eve had left it and tried to relax. Inside, he was reeling. How had they survived the bomb?

When Eve returned from the bathroom, Michael found himself struggling to concentrate on the conversation. He made his excuses and went home. Could he use what he now knew to his advantage, and gain Tommy’s trust?

Chapter 10

Daniel

Daniel's journey to Palermo to visit Jack was all thanks to meeting Eve in Madrid. He was happy to have his family back and even happier to have rekindled his relationship with Anna. It had taken time and lots of conversations. Over time, the two had fallen in love again; in fact, they were stronger than ever. They shared the memories and trauma of their escape from the *Lucky Lady*. It had brought the family closer together and Eloise and Leah were delighted to have their father back in their lives.

Daniel was apprehensive about seeing Jack again. He wondered how advanced his dementia now was. He felt himself bracing for what he might find.

Once he had signed the care home visitors' register, the receptionist led him to Jack's room and asked him to wait. She explained that Jack was in a talking therapy group. Daniel sat down and took a deep breath. He wondered if Jack would recognise him.

When the nurse led Jack into the room, Daniel did a sharp intake of breath. He was shocked at how much Jack appeared to have aged in such a short space of time. He stood up to greet him.

"Jack, how are you?" he asked, his eyes welling up as he helped Jack into a seat. Jack studied him warily and said nothing.

"How has he been?" Daniel asked the nurse, impatient to

know the state of his friend's health.

"Jack doesn't say much these days," the nurse told him gently. "His health has taken a decline since you would have last seen him. He now needs help dressing, bathing and with the toilet. But we have round-the-clock care and Jack is in a safe place and well looked after. Aren't you, Jack?" She smiled at the old man. Jack nodded but looked absent and did not speak. The nurse left the room, closing the door gently behind her.

"Jack, I'm so sorry it's taken me so long to visit you," Daniel said in a rush, gripping Jack's hands in his own. "Something happened. Anna and the girls came down to Mondello to visit. When she was here, Tommy came to the villa to thank me for looking after Eve while he was out of town. Do you remember Tommy and Eve?" Jack stared absently ahead, rocking slightly to and fro on his chair.

Daniel continued, desperate to explain. "Well, it turns out Tommy is Reggie's brother. Can you imagine? He had tracked us down to avenge Reggie's death." Daniel didn't know if Jack was listening or understood but he continued. "Eve came to our rescue and we managed to escape. We're living in Madrid for the time being. We unexpectedly ran into Eve a couple of weeks ago. I knew it was high time I paid you a visit. Jack can you hear me? Do you understand what I'm saying? Squeeze my hand if any of this makes sense," he pleaded, sighing loudly.

They sat in silence, Daniel gazing pleadingly at Jack's face. And after a few moments, Jack gave him the slightest of squeezes. Daniel's eyes filled with tears.

"Oh Jack, I'm so sorry for leaving you here. Your illness, not coming to visit you… All of it. You're never out of my thoughts, please know that," and Daniel found himself sobbing. Jack gently laid his hand on Daniel's bowed head. Daniel knew without words that Jack understood and forgave him, and he sobbed still harder.

The emotional moment was interrupted by the receptionist popping her head round the door.

"I'm sorry to interrupt," she said. "Could you come down to reception please?" Daniel glanced questioningly at her blank expression.

"Yes, of course," he replied, "Are we all paid up? There's not a problem with the funding, is there?" But the receptionist had disappeared again.

Daniel put his arm around Jack and squeezed his shoulder. "I'll be back soon," he told him and made his way back to reception.

He stopped short when he was approached by two armed officers.

"Steven Arnold – or, rather Daniel Edgar – you are under arrest for the murder of Reggie Raymond Brown," one told him, pulling his arms around behind his back and cuffing him, then pushing him forward through the doors to the waiting police car. His head was pushed down and he was shoved into the back seat.

Daniel felt himself sink with defeat.

Chapter 11

Anna

At Daniel's arrest, Anna did not let her devastation overcome her. She packed up the house in Madrid and made arrangements for her and the girls to return to Britain, as soon as they possibly could. The girls were inconsolable. They had only just got used to having their father back in their lives and now he had been cruelly taken away from them again, and for what reason? To be sent to jail! They were desperate to get back to see their friends and grandparents.

Their friends and grandparents were all looking forward to their return home; even under such terrible circumstances. The salon had kept her place open, knowing only that Anna had gone abroad to patch up her marriage and would be back. Her parents had been renting out her house while she was away. They prepared rooms in their own home in Wales, where Anna and the girls could stay until the tenants moved out.

Anna's parents met her and the girls at the airport. Anna clung to her mother and surprised even herself by the force of her tears. They drove straight back to the house.

"Oh, Mum," cried Anna when the girls had gone to bed. "What a mess." She told them the whole story, including the part where Reggie had appeared in their lives and destroyed their marriage. She told them all about Daniel and Jack and their art forgeries. How, when Daniel met Reggie again, he had threatened to expose him. She told them of the dreadful decision Daniel had taken to push him in front of a bus. She told them how Daniel had been living in Mondello with Jack, when they went to visit him. She explained how Tommy had arrived to carry out his revenge plan.

Anna's parents were horrified. They had been under the impression Anna had gone to Sicily to patch up her marriage – but to discover their son-in-law was a murderer… And that their own daughter and grandchildren had been so close to death… But it certainly made sense of the marriage breakdown and Daniel's disappearance.

Exhausted, Anna climbed the stairs to her old bedroom. She was happy to be home with her parents. She had missed them sorely the whole time she had been in Madrid. Tomorrow she was going to visit Daniel in prison, to hear how he was faring and what sentence he was likely to get. It was so unfair. They had just found each other again and had been living a fairly happy life. Now they were home but separated again. Anna did not know what the future held for them and cried herself to sleep.

Chapter 12

Tommy

When Tommy's father called him to say the police had been round to inform him they had arrested a man for Reggie's murder, Tommy sat down abruptly.

When he found out it was Daniel Edgar who had been arrested, he was even more shocked. How could a man who had been dead for five years be arrested for murder?

Michael was sitting on his father's couch listening to the phone conversation and when Tommy hung up, he cleared his throat.

"I was about to tell you about Daniel – I saw a photo of him and Anna on Eve's phone."

"What? Why didn't you tell me this before?" And Tommy's eyes flashed angrily.

"I never got the chance till now," protested Michael. "I swear, Dad, I was about to tell you."

"Has she been in touch with him this whole time?" Tommy asked.

"I've no idea," Michael replied, shaking his head, "I didn't ask. I wanted to tell you first, see what you wanted to do about it."

"This is unbelievable," said Tommy. "You need to work on Eve and get her to see me. I need to know if she's been in touch with him this whole time."

"I'll get on it," said Michael, "I promise, Dad, I'll make her see you again."

Chapter 13

Daniel

Daniel laughed wryly to himself. He, Anna and the girls were all back in the UK; but not together. He had spoken to a lawyer and had explained the whole story. Daniel didn't see any point in lying now and chose to be as honest as possible.

The lawyer promised Daniel he would do his best to get a reduced sentence but told him he should prepare himself for prison. There was no way he was going to walk away from this. Daniel felt oddly relieved. He would be punished for his crime and, at the end of it all, he would be a free man. He could live back in Yorkshire, hopefully with his family. He would finally be able to stop looking over his shoulder.

∞

At visiting time, he sat at the table waiting for Anna to arrive. When the visitors were let in, he cried at the sight of her and hugged her briefly before a guard snapped, "No physical contact."

"How have you been?" Anna asked him tearfully.

"I'm okay, I'm fine," he assured her. "You know, being arrested, being tried for Reggie's murder, this might be the best thing that's happened to me. I'll serve my time. Be punished for what I did."

"But how long will you be locked up?" Anna sobbed. "We

only just got our lives back."

"Not really," he said sadly. "We would always be looking over our shoulders, living a lie. Who's to say Tommy wouldn't come looking for us again? At least this way I'm being held accountable. You and the girls will be fine. I'm sure of it." He paused, then added, "Will you wait for me, Anna?"

"Of course I will," she answered, looking him straight in the eye. "I could never trust another man after what happened with Michael. Daniel, you are the only man I could ever love. I promise I will wait for you. I will do my best to be a great parent to the girls. We will think about you every single day."

"That's what will get me through this," he told her with tears in his eyes.

Back in his cell, Daniel felt as though a weight had been lifted from him. Ever since Reggie's murder, he had carried the burden of it, and it was a heavy one to bear. He had thought he would never have the opportunity to repent for his sin. But now he would be sent to trial and punished for his crime; then he could start to rebuild his life.

Chapter 14

Eve

Eve was eager to visit Anna as soon as she had returned to Britain. "I will always be here for you," she told Anna as she hugged her tightly. "Whatever you need. I want to be in the girls' lives and offer them support, too." Anna was more than grateful. Eve would be a fantastic support and role model for the girls. And she knew she would need all the help she could get.

When Eve visited Daniel in prison, she repeated the promise she had made to Anna and assured Daniel she meant it. She would do her best for his family, and be there for them through thick and thin. Daniel was relieved and grateful. With Anna being so strong and the girls looking up to Eve as a role model, he knew he could face whatever lay ahead.

"I'm quite glad I was arrested," Daniel told Eve. He laughed at her look of puzzlement. "Killing Reggie was so drastic, I've never got over it. It's haunted me ever since. This way, I'll be properly punished."

Eve nodded. "You just need to get through this," she said. "When you're finally free, you can begin your life again. I just hope your sentence is not too severe."

Chapter 15

Michael

Michael chose to go ahead and help smuggle the stolen jewellery for the men he had recently been introduced to. He didn't know a lot about them but the returns he would make made the job hard to turn down. He knew nothing about how they came into possession of the jewellery and he did not want to. His job was to conceal the goods in one of his dad's company vehicles which would be 'sold' to someone in France. It would be transported by ferry and picked up in France, where the jewellery would end up in the right hands to be sold on.

It was a piece of cake, thought Michael. He decided not to tell Tommy at all. He would get his cut, which would be fairly substantial, and if all went well he would continue working this way. Maybe one day he would be financially strong enough to go it alone. It would be a relief not to be under his father's control.

Thinking of his father, he made his way to Eve's house. It was time to put into action his plan to get her back into Tommy's life.

She made a pot of coffee and they sat down on the couch together.

"So, they arrested Daniel for Reggie's murder." Michael got straight to the point, and watched his sister closely to see her response.

"So I believe," Eve answered calmly.

"It's strange, don't you think? We thought they had all died in the explosion," he continued.

"Well, thank God they didn't," Eve said, setting her cup down on the table.

"Did you know they were still alive?" asked Michael, deciding to just come out with it.

"No, of course not," lied Eve, colouring slightly.

"I saw pictures of you with Daniel and Anna on your phone so stop lying, Eve," Michael said flatly.

Eve froze, then turned to look at him. "Okay, I did know they were alive, but I only just found out. When I went to Madrid for my fashion show, I saw Daniel and Anna at a market. It was purely coincidental. But I went back to their house and they explained what happened.

"Dad had been smoking on the *Lucky Lady* and Daniel could smell the stale smoke. He suspected Dad had been there. They jumped off the boat and swam to safety. To cut a long story short, they ended up in Madrid, where they have been living ever since. Daniel went to visit Jack in Palermo, where he was arrested for Reggie's murder. Apparently, the police had received an anonymous tip-off after the *Crimewatch* programme. The caller told them all about Jack and also told them he was living in Sicily with Steve Arnold – Daniel Edgar. That he was the man who had pushed Reggie in front of the bus. The police searched Mondello and Palermo for Daniel. Thanks to Dad, they had escaped to Madrid, where they knew nothing of the police investigation. But the police suspected Daniel would at some point return to visit Jack. It took five years but return he did, and that is why he is now awaiting trial."

Michael said nothing about his relief that Anna and the girls had survived. And while he would have been happy to see Daniel dead, at least he had been arrested; at least he would have to serve time and would not escape punishment.

"Dad's not well," he suddenly said. Time for the plan to be put in place.

"So?" she said, taking a small jar of nail polish and painting her toenails.

"No, I mean really not well. He is in agony with his stomach," Michael told her convincingly.

"So, he should go to the doctor," she said, unsympathetically.

"Yes, he is, he's going next week." Michael adopted a look of concern. "What if it's something serious, Eve? Don't you think it's time you let him back into your life? What if you leave it too late? How would that make you feel?"

"It would make me feel nothing, Michael. I can't associate with someone who felt nothing about taking the lives of a family, no remorse, no nothing," Eve was getting upset now, thinking about what her father had attempted to do.

"But they're still alive," Michael reminded her.

"No thanks to Dad," she said tartly.

Michael sighed and stood up. "Okay, well I better go. I said I'd pop in on Dad. He's gravely ill, Eve. Just think about it, that's all I'm asking. I could use your help caring for him, if nothing else." Eve said nothing but showed her brother to the door, saying goodbye with a hug.

She padded back into the living room. Sitting down again, she leaned back and thought about her father. He had done so much for them growing up. He was her biggest cheerleader in life, and she had to admit she had missed him. Maybe it was time to bury the hatchet.

Chapter 16

Daniel

On the day of Daniel's sentencing, Anna and her parents made their way to court. The trial had gone on for three weeks. The jury had heard all mitigating circumstances. They heard about Reggie's lust for revenge, his attack on Anna, the robbery at the farmhouse where Daniel's involvement had been coerced. The art frauds, the moment of Reggie's death. Daniel and Jack escaping to Palermo. They had heard it all – everything except Tommy's arrival and his failed murder attempt. Daniel had not told his lawyer about that. He did not want to implicate Eve and kept his silence to protect her.

The jury had deliberated for more than a day and had found it difficult to reach a verdict. Some were of the mind that anyone in those circumstances would have done the same thing. Others believed it was wrong to take a life no matter what. As the jury returned to their seats, the tense silence in the court was almost suffocating.

"Ladies and gentlemen of the jury, have you reached a unanimous decision in the case of Daniel Edgar, who stands accused of the murder of Reggie Raymond Brown?" asked the judge.

"We have, your honour," answered the foreman.

"Then please tell the court what verdict you have arrived

at."

"We the jury find the defendant Daniel Edgar guilty of voluntary manslaughter," reported the foreman, before taking his seat.

The judge addressed the court. "To sum up, the jury have found you, Daniel Edgar, guilty of the lesser charge of voluntary manslaughter. We have heard all the circumstances leading up to the death of the victim. Some might argue you were indeed provoked into the actions you took on that fateful day. We have heard your remorse for your actions and your willingness to serve the penalty that your crime must dictate. In this case, a prison sentence is in order. This is a serious crime. I sentence you, Daniel Edgar, to six years in prison, to be served at Her Majesty's pleasure. I would like to thank the jury for their time. I appreciate this has been a stressful and emotional case to judge."

Daniel was white as a sheet as he was led from the dock. He did not look at anyone and kept his head down. There were cheers from Reggie's family; his father and nephew were there. Tommy was not in attendance. Anna and her parents remained in their seats, unsure if this was a good or bad outcome. They waited to speak to Daniel's lawyer, to find help in understanding what just happened.

"This outcome is better than I'd hoped," he told Anna and her parents. "If the jury had issued a verdict of murder, it would have been a far more severe sentence. Voluntary manslaughter means the jury thought Daniel had been sufficiently provoked into taking the actions he did that day, which therefore lessened the sentence. With good behaviour, Daniel should be out in less than four years." Four years seemed a long time but she could cope with that, Anna thought as she walked away from the court with her parents. She would be busy with work and the girls and she would visit Daniel every week. Once he was home, they could start to rebuild their lives. Anna was determined to remain positive. There was no other option.

Chapter 17

Eve

Eve visited Anna and the girls in their own home, since the tenants had found another place.

"How are you coping?" she asked Anna, accepting the mug of coffee and warming her slender fingers.

"I'm fine now," Anna replied, sitting beside her at the table. "We always knew he would have to serve time. I think Daniel had accepted that. In fact, he was glad to finally face up to what he had done. Reggie was a bad man but no-one deserves to be murdered."

"Well, I think that's very generous of you, considering what he did," Eve told her.

"Yes, but Daniel has been in turmoil ever since. I can't wait for him to get home so we can rebuild our lives without looking over our shoulder the whole time. Your dad… do you think he will still be seeking revenge?"

"I would hope not but I've actually no idea. I don't speak to him now," Eve replied. It made her think, though; maybe she should make up with her dad, if only to keep an eye on him and make sure he wasn't planning anything else to hurt her friends.

Michael called her just as she got home from Anna's. "Eve, I really think you should see Dad. He's in a bad way. You might have noticed that he wasn't at the hearing." He sounded serious and Eve thought she might regret it if she didn't go now.

"Okay, I'll be over in half an hour," she replied, throwing her coat back on and grabbing her keys. She was apprehensive but Tommy not having been at Daniel's sentencing meant he must be ill.

Michael let her into their father's house. "He's upstairs," he said solemnly. Eve hung up her coat and made her way up to their father's bedroom. She knocked softly at the door. She was not sure what state she would find her father in.

"Dad, it's me," she said, entering the room. Tommy was in bed, covers pulled up to his neck. There was a glass of water on his bedside table with a selection of different painkillers.

"Eve," he said weakly. "Thanks for coming, it's been so long since I've seen you. I missed you." She sat awkwardly on the side of the bed and took his hands in hers.

"What are the doctors saying?" she asked, looking at the different painkillers on the table. "What are they saying is wrong with you?"

"They don't know, bloody quacks," he said. He had always told his family not to trust doctors, and he played on Eve knowing that. "All I know is my stomach hurts. I've not eaten for days and I feel so weak."

"Maybe it's punishment for what you did in Mondello," Eve said, looking him straight in the eye.

He glanced away. “They escaped, didn’t they?” he asked sullenly. “Thankfully, now Daniel’s where he should be. Thinking he could murder my brother like that and walk away scot-free…” Eve noticed her father’s voice getting stronger.

And a hammering on the front door saw him sit up in bed, all sign of weakness gone.

“Police! Open up!” Eve looked at her dad in fear as they heard the shout downstairs.

“What the hell?” Tommy leapt out of bed. He was dressed in trousers and a shirt and Eve stared at him. He wasn’t unwell at all. What was he playing at? But before she could ask him, Tommy was running down the stairs. She stood on the landing and watched him fling open the front door.

“Thomas Brown, you are under arrest for the smuggling of stolen jewellery,” a police officer immediately walked into the hallway and grabbed Tommy by the arm. “You do not have to say anything. But it may harm your defence if you do not mention when questioned something which you later rely on in court. Anything you do say may be given in evidence.”

An officer took hold of Michael, who had appeared from another room, and repeated the charge. Father and son were both handcuffed, while Eve stood silent, with her hand to her throat. What had they done now?

“Michael,” Tommy snarled. “What the hell have you been

up to?"

Michael said nothing as the pair were led away in handcuffs and driven off in waiting police cars.

Chapter 18

Michael

They were driven to the police station in separate cars, much to Michael's relief. But his peace didn't last long. When he arrived at the station, Tommy was already there, shouting at the officers and demanding to know why they had been arrested.

"One of your cars was spot searched on its way to France," an officer told him. "Stolen jewellery, with an estimated value of over a million pounds, was found concealed in the boot. Though not that well concealed," he added with a smirk.

"That's impossible," said Tommy, looking puzzled. "I know nothing about this."

"Maybe your son can fill you in," laughed the officer, but as Tommy turned angrily towards Michael, he was led away to a cell.

Michael joined his father in the cell when he had been signed in, and Tommy unleashed his fury. "What the hell have you been up to? Tell me the truth." His eyes were ice cold.

"I'm sorry," Michael replied lamely. "I was going to give you a share of the cut," he added, as if this was going to make any difference now.

"Who have you got yourself involved with?" asked Tommy.

"Just some new faces. They said it was easy money."

Michael felt small and stupid now. He should have listened to Tommy. No new faces.

"What have I always told you?" Tommy raged. "Trust no-one new. I have dealt with the same people all my working life, and never once have I found myself in this position. Now, because of your stupidity, we are facing jail time." Michael sat in silence and Tommy's anger seemed to burn out. They were here now. There was nothing they could do about it. Tommy, too, sat down and both men became lost in their own thoughts about what lay ahead.

∞

Since Michael had no intention of ratting out his accomplices, he knew he would be in trouble. After his "No comment" responses to every police question, their lawyer told them they would definitely be facing a jail sentence and that they should prepare themselves.

The robbery of the stolen jewellery had been a violent one. The shop owner had sustained life-threatening injuries. Because it could not be proven that either Tommy or Michael was involved in the robbery, they were each sentenced to two years in jail.

Chapter 19

Daniel

Daniel returned to his art to keep him occupied in prison, and he was happily surprised to find that, as in the army, his artistic skills made him some friends. Even the hardest of criminals gave him pictures of their wives, girlfriends or kids to draw. He delighted them with the portraits he produced, so real and lifelike. Even the prison guards had him paint for them. He was kept busy by the number of requests he was getting.

The first night of his incarceration, he was horrified to find he would be sharing a cell with a prisoner known as 'Slasher', who was inside for life for slashing the throats of people who had got in his way. He was a gang member and had lived an entire life of crime and violence. He was a big man, with an unsightly scar on his throat which ran from ear to ear. He had been attacked and had had his own throat slit, though not forcefully enough to have killed him. Since that day, all his violent attacks were delivered by the same means – but he made sure he cut deep enough to do the job. He was the prison's most notorious criminal and everyone feared him, even the screws. On his first night inside, Daniel slept with one eye open.

But his creative talents meant he got even Slasher on side. The formidable criminal commissioned Daniel to paint all the members of his family and even his dog. Daniel happily complied; if it meant being in Slasher's good books he would do it, willingly.

It wasn't long before Daniel was moved into a cell with a young guy called Patrick, who was doing time for petty thieving. He was chilled out and in no way as threatening as Slasher had been. Slasher's mood could change in seconds. He'd go from laughing and chatting to slicing off a prisoner's fingers in the dinner hall if they said the wrong thing. Although Daniel was in Slasher's good books for now, he still felt at risk sharing a cell with the unpredictable man. Walking into Patrick's cell, Daniel felt overwhelmingly relieved.

∞

When a new group of prisoners were brought into the common area, Daniel tensed and his stomach turned over at the sight of Tommy and Michael among them. Had they planned this? Was this really how far they would go to exact their revenge? His heart sank. It was impossible to avoid other people in this place. There was nowhere to hide and it was inevitable they would come face to face fairly soon.

And sure enough, as Daniel sat eating his dinner, Tommy and Michael slammed their trays down opposite him.

"So, you escaped the *Lucky Lady*?" Tommy snarled at him, his eyes blazing.

"Yes, we did," answered Daniel boldly. "What the hell

where you thinking, trying to murder my wife and daughters?"

"You thought nothing of killing one of my family," Tommy answered.

"He ruined my life," Daniel snapped, angry at being reminded of Reggie. "It was a moment of madness, and I regretted it. I only wanted him out my life and to stay away from me. But he was never going to do that."

"So you thought you'd just push him in front of a bloody bus. My little brother, with his whole life ahead of him. You broke my father's heart." Daniel could feel the hatred Tommy had for him. He stood to leave, lifting his tray, but as he turned Tommy snarled again.

"Watch your back," he said threateningly. And the words affected him just as Tommy had hoped they would – Daniel returned to his cell feeling physically sick.

Daniel glanced at Patrick as he entered the cell. The young lad was lying on the bottom bunk reading a book. Daniel stood in the centre of the small room, and Patrick glanced up at him.

"What's up?" he asked, studying Daniel's pale face.

"My past has come back to haunt me. Again," Daniel told him.

"That's right. It has," came a voice behind him, and Daniel spun round to see Tommy and Michael standing in the doorway. "Get out," Tommy gestured to Patrick. Patrick, easily intimidated, jumped off the bunk and did as he was told. He was barely through the door before Michael slammed it shut.

"I can't let you get away with murdering my brother," Tommy told Daniel.

"I'm not getting away with it," Daniel pleaded. "I'm doing time for it."

"A poxy six years. You're likely to be free in four and that's not enough," Tommy said, inching closer. He grabbed the pillow from Patrick's bunk and pushed it over Daniel's face, shoving him backwards till he fell onto the bed. Daniel fought but the older man's strength was almost inhuman. The more Daniel struggled, the harder Tommy pushed down on him and the more exhausted Daniel became. He felt hotter and fainter and weaker, as Michael held down his legs and Tommy used all his weight to push the pillow down over his face.

Chapter 20

Anna

Anna, following Tommy and Michael's sentencing in the news, was horrified to discover they would be heading for the same jail as Daniel. She knew it would not be long before Daniel came to some sort of harm at their hands. She rang Eve and begged her to visit her father and plead with him to leave Daniel alone. Eve did not hesitate to agree. Maybe she could convince her father she would be back in his life when he got out – but only if he left Daniel alone. It was worth a shot and Eve would do anything to ensure Daniel's safety. The family had been through so much at the hands of her father it was the least she could do.

When Anna had visited Daniel in prison he was in fairly good spirits. He told her he was popular with the other prisoners because of his drawings and she had been so relieved that he was managing to cope. She felt she could be optimistic that they would get through this together; weather the storm and come out the other side. But now she could not sleep. Her nights were splintered by jagged nightmares of Tommy attacking Daniel, each dream a different scenario and each just as terrifying as the last.

When she took the call from the prison her heart sank. And when she heard that there had been "an incident", a cold shiver engulfed her whole body.

Chapter 21

Daniel & Anna

Daniel could feel the change in atmosphere even before he opened his eyes. When he woke, he could see a police officer standing guard outside his hospital room; he also saw that he was attached to a ventilator helping him breathe.

The bleep of the monitor sped up as he felt his heart beat a little faster. But he was too drowsy to move, and he only watched as a young nurse came into the room.

"Ah, hello, Mr Edgar, you're awake!" she said happily.

"What happened?" Daniel asked. His brain felt muddy and he had no idea why he was here.

"I'll get Dr Fields to explain what's happened to you," the nurse told him gently. "You're in the hospital. Don't try to move or get out of the bed. You'll likely be feeling very wobbly and you are attached to a lot of machines." Daniel closed his eyes. His head hurt like hell, and his thoughts were cloudy and unreal. He had no memory of how he got here.

"Mr Edgar," Dr Fields, a woman in her forties, entered the room. "It's great to see you awake."

"What's happened? Why am I here?" Daniel asked her.

"You were attacked in your cell," said Dr Fields smoothly. "Someone tried to suffocate you. You blacked out from lack of oxygen. We will have to carry out tests to make sure there is no permanent damage. The fact that you have woken up and are talking to me right now is a fabulous start," she added.

"Attacked? Who would attack me and why?" Daniel struggled to break through the fog in his mind.

"You are probably suffering from temporary memory loss due to your ordeal," Dr Fields sidestepped the question. "We will keep you here for observation, until we have carried out more tests and are able to make an informed assessment. For now, rest and recuperate, Mr Edgar. Ring the bell if you need anything. Do not attempt to get out of bed – you are attached to many drips and machines."

It was an unnecessary warning – Daniel was asleep again before she had left the room.

∞

When Anna arrived at the hospital, she spoke to Dr Fields before visiting Daniel.

The doctor reassured her. "Thankfully, it seems Daniel's brain was not starved of oxygen long enough for it to do any permanent damage. But further tests will have to be carried out before that can be confirmed. He is suffering from what we hope is short-term memory loss. In most cases such as this, the memory returns to normal after a period of time. We need to keep him in hospital for further observation, before he can go back to prison."

"Okay," said Anna, nodding and swallowing her tears.

"But I don't want him ever to go back to that prison where he was nearly murdered." She was openly sobbing now.

"Go and wash your face before you see him," suggested the doctor, kindly. "You have to be strong for Daniel."

"Yes," Anna nodded again, and she made her way to the bathroom, where she could wash her face and paint on a fake smile.

Anna sat with Daniel until he woke up. She tried to ignore the police officer standing in the corner of the room – it only reminded her Daniel was still a prisoner. She went over and over in her mind what she had learned had happened, picturing the scene and feeling sick. Tommy and Michael would have killed Daniel if another inmate – called Slasher! – had not intervened and pulled Tommy off. She thanked God for Slasher and prayed that Daniel would make a full recovery.

"Anna." She was pulled from her thoughts by Daniel's weak voice. He looked groggy and he cautiously massaged his forehead. "Can you pass me a drink of water?" Anna held the plastic cup to his lips so he could take a sip. Then his head sank heavily to the pillow again.

"What happened to me? Why am I here?" Daniel asked.

"Don't you remember?" Anna said gently. "The warden told me you were attacked. Tommy tried to suffocate you in your cell." Anna gazed at Daniel's face, looking for signs that he remembered the attack.

"Tommy? How did he get into the prison?" Daniel looked blank.

"Tommy and Michael were put in the same prison as you, after they got arrested for smuggling goods. Don't you remember seeing them?" Anna tried to dampen down her concern. She remembered what the doctor had told her about memory loss.

"No, I don't." But Daniel seemed too dazed to be concerned about his lack of memory.

"Don't worry too much," Anna reassured him. "The doctor said your memory should return in time. Just concentrate on getting better."

"I don't have much choice in the matter," Daniel replied, looking woozy and blank.

Chapter 22

Eve

Eve was both furious and dismayed by her father and brother's attempt on Daniel's life. She had planned to warn them not to hurt him but she was too late. She knew from their solicitor that they were moved to another prison and would each receive added time to their sentences for the attempted murder. She was finished with them both. She was so grateful that Daniel had survived the attack. If it had ended in his death, she couldn't help feeling she would have been somehow to blame.

Eve spent more and more time with Anna and the girls. She had a fashion show coming up and had invited them to see it, hoping to take their minds off Daniel. There would be a lot of new designers and it promised to be a glittering event. Now that she wasn't focusing so hard on work, Eve decided it was time for her to socialise more, put herself first for a change. She had even agreed to go on a date with an up-and-coming designer she had met during a fashion show.

Lewis Chandler was from Leeds and now lived in London. He had always shown great flare for fashion and, like Eve, had been working solidly for years. His social life had also taken a back seat and now he was ready to spend time on himself. With his blond hair and incredible blue eyes, he and Eve made an attractive couple.

As Eve became more comfortable in his company, and more trusting of him, she told Lewis of all that had happened in the last few years. He was naturally horrified and assured her that he would help her support Anna, Leah and Eloise until Daniel was released.

Chapter 23

Anna

Daniel made a full recovery and was returned to prison, but safe from the hands of Tommy and Michael. They were transferred to a different prison and could no longer hurt him. With the support of her parents, of Rachel and Susan, Eve and Lewis, Anna was managing to hold everything together – just.

Leah was excelling in swimming competitions while studying to become a lawyer. After all her father had gone through, she was intrigued by law and was loving every minute of her new-found passion. She had a boyfriend she met at university. Stuart was studying to become an architect and Anna was very happy with her daughter's choice. She knew Daniel would approve and she could not wait for them to meet one another.

Meanwhile, Eloise qualified as a veterinary nurse and loved her job at a local vet. She got to spend all day with animals and could not be happier. She was a great help to Anna during the years of Daniel's imprisonment and matured quickly. She visited Daniel often and enjoyed hearing the prison stories; well, not all of them. Only the funny ones.

∞

It was four years and twenty-one days before Daniel was finally released. Anna cleaned the house from top to bottom. There was new bedding on the beds, and fresh towels. Eve helped her transform the house into a showpiece. All Daniel's favourite foods were in the cupboards. Beers, wines and spirits were set out and she'd had a gardener come round to landscape the garden – it looked completely different. She had even bought new garden furniture. Finally, everything was ready for Daniel to come home. Anna arranged for a party the following evening – this evening she wanted Daniel to herself, and she was sure he would appreciate this, too. He would need a day to come to terms with his new freedom.

Chapter 24

Daniel

The day of Daniel's release finally arrived. He said his farewells to the prisoners he had become friends with and wished them all well. He wanted to hug Slasher but settled for thanking him again for saving his life. A hard man not prone to emotional outbursts, Slasher had tears in his eyes.

"You're a good man, Daniel, you should never have been in here," he said gruffly. "You've raised everyone's spirits and we've all got a bit of you in the paintings you did for us. I'll never forget you." Daniel was stunned by the emotional speech and shook Slasher's hand hard.

"Take care mate," he said as he took his final look back at what had been his home for the last four years.

Anna was waiting for him outside the gates. She ran into his arms and they clung together for several moments before he got into the car and she drove him home. This time he did not look back.

Daniel was blown away at the work Anna had done to make their home so beautiful. It was luxurious. He guessed correctly that Eve had been instrumental in helping with a few things. The first thing he wanted was a leisurely bath and to put some new clothes on.

Anna left him to relax while she made him a tasty supper.

An hour or so later Daniel came down wearing a new jersey, joggers and a fresh white t-shirt. He couldn't believe he was home. It was like the weight of the world had been lifted from his shoulders.

He sat down at the beautifully set table and enjoyed the three-course dinner that Anna had prepared for him. He was taken aback by the effort she had gone to. "Here's to us and to new beginnings," he said, lifting his glass in a toast. Anna raised hers and clinked glasses with him. She told him the rest of the family and friends would be joining them the next evening. They were all desperate to see him but, for tonight, it would be just them. That suited Daniel perfectly.

When they finally went to bed, it was like old times. They reaffirmed their love for one another then both slept deeply until late the next morning.

Daniel contacted the care home in Palermo. He was informed that Jack had passed away three months earlier and was buried in a Palermo graveyard. Daniel vowed to visit his old friend's grave, sad that he would never see him again. The last thing he had told him was that he would be back and he never got the chance. He hoped Jack's last years on Earth had not been too hard.

Chapter 25

Tommy & Michael

Prison made Tommy an even harder man. He was angry. Very angry. He had nothing to lose now, knowing that Eve would never talk to him again after his attempt on Daniel's life. He had lost everything he had worked so hard to build up. Michael knew to keep away from him and stay out of his road. They grew apart while in prison. Tommy was furious with Michael and would never forgive him for his failure.

But Michael was too busy making friends with some very seedy characters to care. He loved hearing their stories and was picking up new ideas all the time. When he got out he knew exactly what he was going to do and there was nothing honest about it. He didn't care. He planned to be top dog one day and if it took a life of crime to get there, then a life of crime it would be.

Meanwhile, Tommy's plans for the future were very black indeed.

Chapter 26

Daniel

As he watched the tide gently ebb and flow, Daniel picked up some flat stones that were scattered along the beach. He threw them into the sea and watched them bounce along until gravity took hold and sunk them into the seabed. He had visited Jack's grave and had said his goodbyes. He had visited the care home and thanked the staff and professionals for all the great care they had taken of Jack in his absence. He gave them a sizable donation.

He thought about the course his life had taken and could scarcely believe he had survived it all. But survive he had and he was thankful for it. He was a changed man and was living the life he had always wanted to live. He was teaching art, Anna continued to work at the salon and his girls were thriving.

They would always have a lifelong friendship with Eve anda shared eventful history. The future looked bright, as long as Tommy and Michael remained in prison. Which wouldn't be forever…

THE END

About the Author

KD Bradley lives on the outskirts of Edinburgh with her husband, two teenage children, their ragdoll cat Sonny and border collie Beau.

A writer from a young age, she began her passion for writing by penning funny odes for each member of her large family, being the youngest of seven.

She has attended many creative writing courses and groups and completed The Writer's Bureau home study course.

Contact the author at bradleykd@btinternet.com